LOVE IN THE LIFE OF SPIES

from Berlin to Buenos Aires

Frank Thomas Smith

Cover Art: The Kiss
Artist: Gustav Klimt, [Austrian, 1862-1918]
Year: 1907-08
Material: Oil and Gold on Canvas
Where: Österreichische Galerie, Vienna
Notes: An Art Nouveau celebration of Love. A man leaning over and kissing a kneeling woman. All shrouded in symbolically patterned gold leaf. A bed of flowers is below them.

Frank Thomas Smith
Visit his website at SouthernCrossReview.org

Cover designed by James D. Stewart

Printed in the United States of America

First Printing: February 2023
Anthroposophical Publications
https://AnthroposophicalPublications.org/

ISBN-13 978-1-948302-51-7 Paperback
978-1-948302-52-4 eBook

She was beautiful in appearance, and was very lovely to behold ... No one spoke ill of her, for she feared God with great devotion.

– Judith 7/8

Table of Contents

Foreword

Florida, Buenos Aires, Argentina

Cerrado read the sign hanging slightly askew inside the upper glass part of Die Glocke's door. What the hell, Jacks thought, it's lunch time, how can they be closed. Something's wrong. He peered through the glass and saw the old waiter sitting alone at a table reading the Freie Presse, a fascist German-language daily. He knocked on the window. The waiter looked up, startled and stared wide-eyed at the door. When he recognized Marvin Jacks he put down the paper, smiled, stood up heavily and opened the door after unlocking it.

"You called for a reservation," he said in German, "*nicht wahr?*"

Jacks nodded. "Why is the restaurant closed? Has something happened?"

"Yes, I'm afraid so." He pulled out a chair from the table he had been sitting at. "Please sit down, Herr Jacks, I have a *mensaje* for you from Frau Marie," he said in "Belgrano-Deutsch," a mixture of German and Spanish used by long time German residents. Jacks remained standing while the waiter hurried into the kitchen and returned immediately clutching a piece of notebook paper. He smiled. "They let her write it when she said it was instructions for picking up her daughter at school. They told me to translate it. They are really stupid, because if it was for me, which she said it was, why would she have to write it out. Anyway, here it is." Jacks read it. *Herr Jacks, Bitte, holen Sie meine Tochter von der Schule ab, um ein-uhr: Rudolf-Steiner-Schule, Warnes 1331.* She signed it: *Marie Clement*

"She told me to give it to you," the waiter said.

"What happened? Where is she? What's your name, by the way?"

"Knoblauch – Federico Knoblauch," the waiter answered, somewhat intimidated by Jacks' height and staccato questions. He, like us all, wanted to be loved.

"Tell me what happened, Federico."

"They came about an hour ago and took Frau Marie and Herr Clement."

Jacks sat down to calm himself. The waiter considered it a friendly gesture and sat across from him.

"Who took them?"

The waiter shrugged: "S.I.D.E., you know, state security. They didn't say so, but you could tell by the green Falcon they parked outside, everyone knows that. Herr Clement went out the back door, but one of them was waiting out in the back, he must have entered through the neighbor's garden, and brought him back in. He said he had gone out for a breath of fresh air, but I think he was trying to get away. Are you a friend of theirs? I remember seeing you here once."

"Yes, a friend."

"Will you pick up their daughter like she asks in the note?"

Jacks look at his watch: 12:45. "Yes, of course. It's almost one, I'll have to hurry."

"What do you think will happen?" the waiter asked, wringing his hands. "What should I do?"

"It's probably a mistake," Jacks said. "You might as well go home and check here tomorrow to see if they've returned."

"But what if they haven't returned?"

Jacks stood up, said *"Auf Wiedersehen, danke,"* and strode to the door.

"Ich danke Ihnen, señor," the waiter said as he let Jacks out.

The Rudolf Steiner Schule stood out in the neighborhood because of its unusual design – nothing square, not even the windows. The place looked like it had been built by a drunken bricklayer. Yet somehow it was attractive, stimulating. Jacks walked into the room marked *Oficina* and handed the note to an oldish, hard-looking matron who read it myopically. She took off her reading glasses and stared at him a moment, then went into the corridor and called out, "Herr Schmidt-Kersmecke!" Jacks looked around the small room cluttered with files and books, all in German. A large photo of a serious looking gent stared down at him from the wall over the lady's desk: Rudolf Steiner the name under it indicated. A few moments later she returned followed by a tall thin elderly man with gray hair touching his shoulders, in a black suit with a black silk flowing artist's bow-tie. Jacks glanced back at the photo and saw the same tie on Steiner.

"Please have a seat, Herr Jacks," he said in German.

"No thanks, I'm in a hurry really, must make a phone call."

"You can use our phone if you like." Jacks hesitated. "Frau Fintelfink and I will be glad to step outside while you're calling."

They left the room and Jacks dialed Panam. John Armstrong was the manager of Panam and a local CIA agent The secretary told him that John Armstrong was at a meeting.

"Get him on the phone, Bea, it's urgent."

"He's not here, it's a Board of Airline Representatives meeting."

"Ok, give me the B.A.R. number, I don't have my address book with me."

"Oh, it's not at the B.A.R."

"Where is it then?"

"At the Sheraton Hotel?"

"The Sheraton? Why there?"

"Every year they have what they call a working lunch at some big hotel. You remember, Mr. Jacks. Mr. Armstrong never comes back to the office afterwards, so I guess they do more than work." She giggled.

"Give me the Sheraton's number, Bea," Jacks said, feeling desperate. She took forever finding it. And it took Jacks forever to finally get Armstrong on the line. "They took them already, John," Jacks began …

"Took who? Who took whom?"

"This phone isn't secure, damn it –"

"Well this one sure as hell isn't either."

"They took the people we're interested in, here in Florida."

"Oh, Frau Marie?"

What an idiot! "Yes, Frau Marie."

"And husband?"

"Yes. Did you do anything to avoid that?"

"Jeez, Marvin, we only talked about it an hour or so ago."

"So, you didn't."

"I couldn't know it was so urgent."

"Well, it is. So please get on it now to release them."

"I'm undercover, Marv, can't do that directly just like that."

"Even to S.I.D.E.?"

"Even to them."

"Your boss at the embassy then."

"He's in Washington."

Jacks took a deep, frustrated breath. "They have telephones in Washington, John. Call him and tell him to get on it. It's easy."

"Well, he might be at important meetings there, and I –"

"This is important. You can't get information from dead people."

"Come on, Marvin, they're not gonna kill East German spies, for god's sake."

"Maybe not ... but everything but. For those guys gang rape is an interrogation method."

"You seem inappropriately concerned, old buddy. The big man'll be back in a few days, and ..."

Jacks stopped listening. Armstrong was right. He shouldn't be so worried, but he was. "Look, John, let's put it this way. Do it for me as a personal favor."

"Don't tell me you got the hots for her already. Man, you're slipping."

"Not already. I knew her from before."

"Before what?"

"Never mind that."

"Whose side are you on anyway, Marvin?"

"Ours … but just do what I ask, and I'll get what you want."

"Like what?"

"Every fucking thing you ever wanted to know about the GDR East German intelligence service. But that's not the point. I'm asking you as a favor, John."

Silence, then: "Okay, I'll do what I can … and you're gonna owe me big, buddy."

He was sitting there with his head in his hands when Herr Schmidt-Something stuck his head in the door. "Are you finished telephoning?"

"Oh … yes, sorry."

Frau Finkelfink pushed in behind him glaring.

"How much do I owe for the calls?"

"Two local calls, eighty centavos," the dragon lady said.

"Oh," Herr S-K said, "I'm sure we can absorb that, Agnes."

"We can't absorb anything, Herbert. "

Jacks fished in his pocket and came up with a peso. "No, she's right, here."

She took the peso and opened a drawer in her desk. She dropped the peso in and started to hand Jacks twenty centavos change. "That's all right," he said generously. It was almost insulting, like offering a tip. She dropped the twenty centavos back in the drawer without a word.

Herr S-K sat down at the table. "I know you're in a hurry, Herr Jacks. At least you said you are. But I've found that most people who say they're in a hurry would be much better off if they weren't, or didn't think there are." Surprised, Jacks was about to answer angrily, but S-K didn't really pause. He smiled and said that Micaela's class had an extra hour today because they were rehearsing for a play. "Personally I think it's somewhat above their age group, but as you probably know, in our schools the teacher is king ... or, rather, queen." He laughed as Jacks frowned. "Actually, I didn't know," he said.

"Well," Herr S-K went on, "Frau Clement must have forgotten to tell you, or forgot herself. Have you known Frau Clement long, Herr Jacks?"

"Yes," Jacks said, surprising himself.

"An interesting woman, don't you agree?"

Marvin Jacks did not tell Herr Schmit-Kersmecke everything that follows below of course, but it did pass through his mind quickly and pictorially as they say when your life passes through your soul directly after death. He did give Herr S-K a radically condensed version though in the hour they spent waiting for Micaela to join them.

1 Paternostro

Judith Baumgartner and Dr. Hans Staudenmaier were huddled over a map of West Berlin in a small basement room with no windows. A long fluorescent light on the ceiling hummed like a beehive. They were preparing a list of objectives that the Soviet Mission Military Patrol was to photograph on its next rounds. Actually, they were suggesting, the Russians would decide. It was frustrating work for they seldom knew if their allies would approve their suggestions. Hans Staudenmaier, a robust middle-aged man with a goatee and rimless glasses, was doing the selecting and dictating to Judith, who made notes in German, which she would later translate into Russian in a stenographer's spiraled notebook made in West Germany. She was young and pretty and intense; there was a certain hardness about her which would have seemed unusual in one so young if we did not know that they were in the building in East Berlin that housed the STASI – East Germany's State Security organization. It was difficult for them to think of objectives in West Berlin that hadn't already been photographed.

Judith looked out the rain-speckled window at a gray sky and, below, the gray city even when the sun was shining. She considered asking the Military Patrol to concentrate on vehicles for a few days, especially military ones, moving or parked. Yes, that was a good idea – but just as she was about to ask Sta,udenmaier, who was the senior person in the section, what he thought of it, a phone rang in an adjoining room and a young man yelled from there: "Fräulein Baumgartner, it's for you." She sighed as though annoyed but was relieved to escape from her Staudenmaier's halitosis for a while at least. It was the Director's secretary on the phone, who told her to go directly to the Herr Direktor Kamerad Wolff's office. The secretary waited only for her to confirm: "Jawohl, Frau Schmidt, aber ..." and hung up before Judith could ask why she was being summoned to such lofty heights. She walked quickly back to Dr. Staudenmaier, "I have to go upstairs, Herr Doktor. Sorry, I'll be back as soon as I can."

"Anything the matter?" he asked, noticing her nervousness, but also curious.

"No." If she said that the Director wanted to see her it would be all over the office in a matter of seconds. She hurried off to the "paternostro," the ancient but reliable dumbwaiter-like elevator, and stepped in like the experienced passenger she was. The paternostro fit only one, so she could wonder in private what the Director, Herr Dr. Wolff, could possibly want with her. She hadn't done anything wrong that she was aware of, but she knew that in the STASI one was not always necessarily aware of one's own wrongdoing. The paternostro was slow, for safety reasons, but it arrived on the fourth floor too soon for her. She wished she wasn't wearing those ugly, but warm, woolen stockings. She knocked on the Director's door and heard Frau Schmidt's hoarse cigarette voice calling her to enter.

"Fräulein Baumgartner?"

"Yes."

Frau Schmidt, dumpy and fiftyish, rose and opened the Director's door behind her. "Fräulein Baumgartner," she announced. Instead of telling Judith to wait, she stood aside as the Director himself came out smiling and took Judith's hand. She thought for a moment that he might kiss it. He was a tall, moderately ugly, middle-aged man with crows-feet behind his eyes from smiling. He wore a double-breasted suit, obviously western made, and was as elegant as any capitalist banker.

"I'm very pleased to meet you, Fräulein Baumgartner," he said, in a surprisingly high voice. "Won't you come in?" Why should he be pleased to meet her? Judith thought. Well, at least he didn't sound as though he was about to fire her. The office was as elegant as he was, and warm. Ah, a fireplace – and burning wood instead of coal. He invited her to sit.

"Coffee or tea?" he asked. She chose coffee. "Bring us two coffees, please, Frau Schmidt," Wolff ordered as he closed the door.

"Now," he said sitting behind his desk across from her, still smiling," you must be wondering why I sent for you."

"Ja, Herr Kamerad Direktor, I was wondering that."

He looked at her for a few moments before going on, studying her pale face, untidy hair and proletarian clothing with approval. "I knew your father," he finally said.

She nodded.

"I was a student of his before ... actually even when the Gestapo arrested him."

"In Leipzig?" It was a stupid question, because it must have been Leipzig, but she felt she had to say something.

"Yes. He was a brilliant man and a dedicated Communist."

"I know," Judith, agreed, "and a good man."

"And that combination – good, a Communist and a Jew to boot, was what doomed him." Judith didn't know if he was being cynical or simply stating an obvious fact. He certainly didn't sound sympathetic. She wondered what had saved Wolff from the same fate. Perhaps he had been none of those things her father was.

"I had no reputation and wasn't a Jew," Wolff said, as though divining her thoughts. "So, I was drafted, but deserted to the Russians." He smiled. "It's an interesting story, but I won't go into it now." Did he intend to go into it later she wondered as Frau Schmidt entered carrying a tray with the coffee things. She poured while they sat in silence. Judith knew from the aroma that the coffee was real.

When his secretary had left, Wolff said, "I'll come right to the point, Fraülein ... May I call you Judith? As your father's friend and the difference in our ages, it doesn't seem incorrect." Judith *Sie* or *Du*? No, that would be too much. "Of course, Kamerad Direktor," she said.

"Good, thank you," he smiled. "How long have you been with us, Judith?"

He must know that, she thought. "A little over a year," she answered.

"Already a year? And I know from the records that you did very well in training and have been doing well in your work as well."

"Thank you."

He nodded. "Cigarette?" He opened a box on his desk. She was about to reach for one, but when she saw that they were Russian *papirosi,* she declined. Wolff laughed. "They *are* awful, aren't they. I only use them to test a person's taste." He reached into his jacket pocket and took out a pack of Marlboros. He offered her one, which she, despite a fleeting notion that it could be a trap, accepted.

"How did you escape from the Nazis, if you don't mind my asking?"

"Not at all. I was sent to the country, to some friends of my father's."

"I see. Gentile friends?"

"Yes."

"And did you change your name – outwardly, that is?"

"I used their family name, and they called me Rotraud."

He smiled, widely this time. "Wunderbar! But frankly I prefer Judith. I believe she was a very strong Biblical personality."

"Yes, she was. She defeated Israel's enemies."

"Did they treat you well, that family I mean, not Israel's enemies?"

Despite his moderate ugliness and his exalted position, Judith found him quite charming. "Yes, very well, and I will always be grateful to them"

"Of course you will."

Wolff looked down at his desk for a moment or so, as though deciding something. "You know, of course, that we have people in the west," he said after lighting his own, then her Marlboro, with a hammer and sickle embossed zippo.

She nodded.

"And, as you can imagine, we don't send just anyone there." He paused as though expecting a reply.

"Of course not," Judith said.

"There are many temptations there – if one isn't a good socialist."

She decided not to say yes and of course to everything he said, so she waited. "Are you a good socialist, Judith?"

"You know that I am, Kamerad Direktor."

The smile was gone now. "How should I know that? Socialism isn't necessarily inherited, you know."

"In my case it is," Judith answered. "I loved my father very much and admired his ideals."

Wolff raised his eyebrows: "Admired?"

"I loved them," she clarified.

"You are speaking in the past tense, Judith."

"I mean when he was alive. I still do and I am a committed Socialist, Kamerad Direktor," she answered, returning his gaze.

"I believe you are, Judith," he said. "Do you take sugar?"

"No, thank you."

"Well, then, please." He picked up his cup and sipped. She followed suit, glad that her hand wasn't shaking. And why should it be? They understood each other and she knew she had passed the test, for whatever purpose it may have been posed.

"Are you really fluent in English?" he asked in English. "Forgive my asking, but I've found that fluency is relative where many of our people are concerned."

"I don't think I am," she replied in English.

He frowned. "Explain, please."

"My English is from studying. I have had little practical experience in the language."

"But it sounds very good to me." He reverted to German. "I didn't expect you to sound like a native speaker."

"Well, I do have an accent."

"Who doesn't? Why did you study it?"

Judith thought for a moment. "A good question; not for practical reasons, I fear. It's just so beautiful."

"I see, and which authors do you prefer?"

A loaded question? But she was prepared: "I like Jack London, but Steinbeck is a better writer."

"Ah – *Of Mice and Men*?"

She smiled for the first time. "Oh yes, and so real, I mean the social conditions he described."

"Hmm, well, one reason is as good as another. And I see from your records that your Russian is fluent" he said in Russian.

"It is," she answered in the same language. "I had Russian teachers in school."

He may have been thinking of asking which Russian writers she preferred, but if so, decided not to. "I have a job for you, Judith," Wolff said. He put three heaping spoonful's of sugar in his cup and drank it down in one gulp.

"In the west, Herr Direktor?" she asked.

"Yes, my dear, in the west." He went to his desk and pushed a button.

"Ja, Herr Direktor?" Frau Schmidt answered.

"Is Herr Cornelius there?"

"Ja, Herr Direktor"

"Send him in, please." He stood facing the door, which opened immediately and a young, tall, well-dressed man entered in an army lieutenant's uniform. He was handsome, too handsome to trust, Judith thought. He stood ramrod straight before Wolff: *"Guten Morgen, Kamerad Direktor Wolff."* Wolff smiled and held out his hand. The other took it, but did not return the smile.

"Now I must introduce you, Stasi style," Wolff said ironically. "Frau Cornelius, meet Lt. Cornelius." Both young people stared at Wolff, speechless. He had expected that reaction, and played his histrionic hand to the hilt. "I must apologize for springing this on you so formally, especially since you, Frau Cornelius, have never heard your new name before. But please, let's relax and sit here." He indicated a couch and easy chairs in the corner of his office. They both hurried to occupy single chairs. "Would you like another cup of coffee, Frau Cornelius?" Judith nodded and Wolff pressed the intercom button on his desk and told Frau Schmidt to bring three more coffees. "And please don't be so stingy with the sugar, Frau Schmidt." He then sat on the couch, crossed his legs, spread his arms over the back of the couch and smiled at them.

When the coffee appeared, almost immediately, and Frau Schmidt had left the room, Wolff became serious. "Here's what we plan for you," he said. "You will receive the necessary training in spy craft and, much easier, the travel agency business. This will take about three months. Then a few weeks in Moscow, theoretically for more training, but in reality for indoctrination and their blessing. How's your Russian, by the way?" he asked, looking at the young man.

"*Gut*, but could be better," the new husband said.

"It will be." Wolf observed them as he offered the real cigarettes, which they accepted, the lieutenant with trembling fingers.

"When you return from Moscow where, according to your story, you met and fell in love, you will get married. Everyone, your families, friends, enemies in case you have any, must be convinced of all this. So, you will look happy, whether you are or not. I sincerely hope that you are, for it would be easier for all concerned, especially you.

"Once you are deemed ready," he continued, "you will defect to West Berlin and report to an American military post. This is a logical step for one of our army officers. You always feel more at home with your peers. Isn't that true, lieutenant?" He didn't wait for an answer. "We don't want you in the hands of West German intelligence or the CIA. American Military Intelligence is stupid and amateurish, which ours is also, by the way; that's why we don't let them handle anything of importance. But the Americans are worse, their various intelligence services compete with each other and very often one doesn't know what the others are doing or what they know. Army intelligence is the worst, mostly because they rotate officers and enlisted men in and out, so that once they have gained sufficient experience to almost know what they're doing, they're gone. There are individual exceptions to this, but they are few and far between and only handle important items and people. You will not be deemed important enough." He drank his coffee slowly but completely and looked at them. "Are you following me so far?"

Both nodded, somewhat hesitantly.

"Good. They will interrogate you, but courteously. You will be treated as guests, VIPs even, most probably at their interrogation center, Camp King, in Oberursel, just outside Frankfurt. You will be cooperative, as behooves defectors seeking a new life in the consumer society."

"What should I tell them, Kamerad Direktor?" Cornelius said.

"Everything. Unless you know some deep dark secrets about us, you won't be able to tell them anything they don't already know. They will want to know about Order of Battle of course, but especially morale. They will question you about our army's morale. You will tell the truth." Wolff looked at Cornelius, waiting for his reaction, which gave the latter the courage to give it.

"Morale isn't really very good, Herr Direktor."

"You don't say," Wolff said, unsurprised. "That's what you will tell them then. They already know it anyway. You must tell the truth about such things so you will not be under suspicion. Understood?"

"Jawohl!"

"Good. Now you, Mrs. Cornelius, they will interrogate you as well, but not with much interest. You have only to confirm your husband's account and tell them about life in East Germany in general, the truth. We have invented an employment for you, in the travel department of the foreign ministry, which will provide a rationale for taking up the same profession in Argentina."

"Argentina?"

"Yes, your penultimate destination. But we'll go into that tomorrow. I have an appointment with the Kamerad Chairman now, and don't want to keep him waiting for more than is his due." He stood up. The others followed suit. "Until tomorrow, then, at nine o'clock here."

"In the morning?" Cornelius asked.

"In the evening," Wolff replied. "You may go now. I suggest you get to know each other." He pressed the intercom button and told Frau Schmidt to call the Chairman's office and advise that he was on his way. He stopped halfway to the door. "By the way, I almost forgot." He grinned. "This is all voluntary of course. I'm afraid I assumed that you would both agree. So, please think it over and let me know what you decide tomorrow. And ... this meeting was secret, top secret in fact, so you are not to mention it to anyone.

As they approached the elevator the lieutenant said to Judith, "The paternostro only holds one at a time, not a good way to get to know each other. So, perhaps we could have a drink somewhere, or ..."

"We should decide first," Judith interrupted him. She felt herself blush. "I mean ... you know ..."

"Yes, of course, I just thought ..." He held his hand out with a slight bow. She shook it and jumped into a paternostro box as it passed. She saw his pressed trousers and gleaming black shoes as she descended. "The next time I see him I will be dressed appropriately," she thought as she glanced down at her woolen stockings.

Back at her desk she ignored the papers and stared into the distance, her heart pounding.

"Is something wrong, Judith?" Staudenmaier asked her.

"What? ... Oh no, it's just that ... that I must leave early today. Is that all right, Dr. Staudenmaier?"

Staudenmaier had asked her several times to call him Hans, but she could never bring herself to do it. He liked to think of himself as fatherly, or at least avuncular, but actually, despite the thirty years difference in their ages, he was quite in love with her. "Yes, of course, but ..." She had already picked up her purse and was heading back to the paternostro before he could finish the sentence.

2 Basic Training

Camp Breckinridge, Kentucky, 1974

Not that we were going anywhere or there was any reason for the march, except that it was in the training schedule: ten-mile night march with weapons and full field pack. That was during one of the hardest parts of the Vietnam war when we were getting the shit kicked out of us by the Vietcong. That meant that there were very few noncoms and officers around to train new guys like us. In fact, we only had the Company Commander, Captain Nugent, who was an Enlisted Man at heart, but couldn't help it if they gave him a battlefield commission for being a hero in Vietnam. He was full of shrapnel and stuff, which must have hurt a lot, so he consumed quite a bit of whiskey – you know, to ease the pain. Then there was First Sergeant Quinn, also a battle-scarred veteran. He ran the company, but I guess First Sergeants run most companies. The Field First Sergeant – the one who did the actual training – was Silas Taylor, a wiry little guy from Georgia who had spent a lot of time in Vietnam, was wounded a few times, and even had a Silver Star. I was surprised – we all were – when I learned that he was only twenty-one years old, because he had eyes that looked a lot older.

There were no more noncoms, except for the mess sergeant, who doesn't count because that's another world, so on the first day First Sgt. Quinn asked if anyone had military experience. No one had, but one guy was a cop in civilian life, so they made him Acting Platoon Leader. Another guy was a lifeguard at Jones Beach, so they made him one too. And so on. I thought of mentioning that I had been a Boy Scout but decided not to. They might have made me Acting Company Commander.

One day during the first week, Field First Sgt. Taylor ran us up a hill. He went first and got there about a hundred yards before the first trainee. We straggled up puffing and groaning and Sgt. Taylor waited until the last one arrived before he began his speech, which went something like this. "Ah said *run* up this here hill and you pussies didn't run, you *crawled*." He didn't shout, just talked loud enough in his southern accent for all of us to hear. Some of us had never even heard a southern accent before, except in the movies. "Now, if y'all keep doin' things that I tell y'all to do like that, I mean crawlin' instead a runnin', you're gonna be fuckin *me*, cause ahm supposed to get this here company in shape to go over and fight the enemy. That means *you-all*. In shape! Now ah don't like to be fucked, and if y'all fuck me, I'm gonna fuck *you-all*. And you can bet your sweet asses that I can fuck y'all better than y'all can fuck me. On the other hand, if y'all do what ah says, and do it *like* ah says, y'all will not have any problems in this here company. Is-that-understood?" Silence. "Answer me, goddammittafuckinhell!" He did shout the last word, if you can call it a word. "Yes, Sergeant," someone mumbled. "Louder! *All* a yuh!" He made us say it louder about five times until we were screaming. "OK, now we're goin' down the hill and we're *runnin'*. If any of you city slickers don't know what runnin' means, I'm telling ya. It means moving *fast*."

Sgt. Silas Taylor had won our respect, and he was as good as his word. A couple of wise guys who thought they could get away with goofing off found themselves on a week of KP; one guy even got sent back to a new company and had to start basic all over again. And when we did things right, we sometimes got off some shit details or got weekend passes.

The first problem with that night march was that Freddy Polanski, the medic, had the flu and couldn't go. Some thought that Freddy had some medical school, because he was pretty good, but I think he just took the three-day first-aid course they give for medics because it was better than the rifle range or some such shit. It wasn't like in the movies, where the medics can practically perform a heart transplant on the battlefield. The second problem was 2nd Lieutenant Scumbag. I forget his real name, but that's what we called him. He simply appeared one day standing alongside Sgt. Taylor when we were in formation. Sgt. Taylor said this is Lt. Scumbag (he used his real name, naturally) and he'll be with us from now on. End of introduction.

"Who wants to be medic until Pvt. Polanski is back on his feet?" Sgt. Taylor asked. We had been in training for two months of the four-month course and had already learned the basic army rule: *never volunteer for anything*. But I wasn't sure that was always a good rule to live by. Look at Sy Abrams. On the first day they asked if anyone knew how to type. Sy raised his hand, and they made him Acting Company Clerk – no lying in the mud at the rifle range, no night marches, no KP. It was from Sy, by the way, that we learned about the argument between Sgt. Taylor and Lt. Scumbag. But I'll get to that later.

I raised my hand, volunteering to be medic. Sgt. Taylor was glad that he didn't have to ask if someone had medical experience and when no one answered just appoint somebody. "OK, Jacks," he said, "Go get Polanski's gear."

Every company has a medic and in combat he doesn't carry his full field equipment, only his first-aid kit and a light carbine rifle instead of the heavy M1. That's so he can run unimpeded to the wounded. His other stuff goes in the truck with the officers' things. As training is supposed to be as realistic as possible, our medic went lightly loaded too. That's why I volunteered. Boy, did I think I was smart!

I'll tell you about the argument now. Just before the march Lt. Scumbag, Field First Sgt Taylor and First Sgt. Quinn were getting some paperwork done in the First Sgt.'s office (actually all they were doing was signing; Sy did all the work) when Lt. Scumbag asked Sgt Taylor if he was going to carry his field pack or put it in the truck. "We ain't got no truck for this march," Sgt. Taylor said. "No truck, no pack."

"Well, Sergeant, I believe in doing everything the men have to do, so we'll be carrying packs, too."

Sgts. Taylor and Quinn looked at him like he was out of his mind.

"I'm sure that Captain Nugent would agree with me," Scumbag added, sensing the coming opposition.

First Sgt. Quinn just laughed and handed a paper to Sy to retype because he didn't like the margins. Sgt. Taylor got red in the face though, especially his eagle-shaped nose, which was a sure sign that he was furious.

"Maybe that's what they teach you college kids in ROTC, but in this here Company A, 101st Airborne Division, we do it *our* way – Loo-ten-int."

Now, sergeants are supposed to obey lieutenants and be respectful, but Sgt. Taylor had just spoken with such dripping scorn in his voice that Lt. Scumbag was ... well ... nonplussed, to say the least. He knew that the sergeant was a Silver Star holder with two combat tours while he, Scumbag, was, militarily speaking, *nada*. But he didn't know that last part yet. What if he ordered Taylor to carry his pack and Taylor told him to fuck off? He couldn't take that chance, so he said *he* would carry his pack and the sergeant could do as he pleased.

"Durned right," Sgt. Taylor agreed. "Anything else, Jack?" he asked Quinn.

"Yeah, how about submitting an application for OCS (Officers Candidate School)?"

Sgt. Taylor didn't miss a beat: "Sure, have Abrams type it up and wipe some general's ass with it." He turned and left quick time while Quinn roared laughing, Sy smirked and Lt. Scumbag looked like a turnip.

Left ... left ... left my wife and forty-nine kids in a starving condition without any gingerbread, thought I did right ... right ... and so on. That's one of the songs we sang while marching through the camp streets. Another one was *Avanti Popolo*, which John Friccero taught us. It was in Italian, so no one except him understood the words. It was only much later, when John and I were in Military Intelligence in Germany and they kicked him out because of his pinko background in college, that I learned it was from the *Communist Internationale*. John said he wasn't really a communist, just sang the song to show how ignorant the army was. He was a college professor, for God's sake. When they kicked him out of M.I. he got a job in Public Information, so he was better off. The whole company sang, shouted rather, *Avanti Popolo* and John sang the rest of the text in his beautiful tenor. We only had to know when to come in again with *Avanti Popolo*.

The soldiers from the other companies always came out to watch us march by. We were the coolest company in the regiment, no doubt about it. We also had a real drummer, a black guy whose first name was J.B. They tried to get him to give his real name, but he insisted that was his real name, he had no other, even had a birth certificate to prove it.

Most of the other companies' drummers just banged on the drum to the marching beat, but J.B. was a jazz drummer and he made marching a pleasure. We skipped, hopped and dragged. Lt. Scumbag was horrified, but Sgt. Taylor, though he didn't skip or hop, tolerated it looking straight ahead with a small smile. We knew he liked it, although he sure as hell didn't know what Avanti Popolo meant.

We marched out of the camp onto a country road. It was a cold clear night and the sky with the stars pinned to it was so low that you felt you could touch it. Sgt. Taylor gave the "walk easy" command. I was alone at the tail end of the four-abreast column walking lightly without a pack and convinced that volunteering was a good idea—sometimes. After a few miles the road narrowed just as the moon came up, giving us the light we would need. Sgt. Silas Taylor had it all figured out, of course. He knew the moon would arrive just when we needed it. He was in the middle and to the left of the column, where he belonged, and Lt. Scumbag bounced along at its head. We compressed ourselves into two columns twice as long from head to ass-end, that is, me.

The road got rougher as we went, but we had already marched it during the day, so we expected that. At about halfway, five miles, the column suddenly stopped and I, night dreaming, bumped into the guy in front of me. A couple of minutes later I heard the cry: MEDIC! Shit, that's me. I ran up along the column to where Lt. Scumbag was waving his arms at me. He, Sgt. Taylor and a group of grunts were huddled around someone sitting on the ground. When they opened up for me to pass, I saw it was Fat Boy, his name was George something. Apparently, he'd stepped on a rock while going downhill and was holding his ankle and grimacing.

"This man is injured, Medic," Lt. Scumbag said, as though I couldn't see that for myself.

I knelt down alongside him and asked what happened. "My fuckin ankle, hurts like hell," he whined. Sgt. Taylor knelt beside me and whispered, "Take off his boot."

"Want me to give him a shot of morphine first?" I asked.

"This ain't the movies, Jacks. You ain't got no morphine anyway. Just take off his boot and act like you know what you're doing."

"Lay down, Fat Boy. I'm going to take off your boot and see what you got."

"Put a blanket under him first," the sergeant said.

I unlaced his boot and pulled it off as gently as I could. You'd think I was amputating the way he squealed. The ankle was red and swollen. I looked in my first-aid kit for the first time and found an elastic bandage. I took it out and looked at Sgt. Taylor, who nodded. So, I wrapped it tightly around Fat Boy's ankle.

"Take the extra socks out of his pack and put them on him," Sgt. Taylor said to someone. "And wrap him in another blanket."

"Yes and use a blanket and two rifles to make a stretcher," Lt. Scumbag interjected. "We can carry him that way."

Sgt. Taylor ignored him. "Popeye!" he yelled down the line.

"Yo," came the answer.

"Get yuh ass over here."

Popeye was a skinny little runt, but the only one in the company who could run faster and farther than Sgt. Taylor, if he was motivated, such as by a direct order.

"Run," Taylor told him. "And ah mean run back to camp, to the hospital, and tell them to send a ambulance here. Tell them it's serious, a man down, or they'll finish their hand of poker before deciding to leave. You come with them so the dumb bastards don't get lost. Got it?"

"Got it, Sarge." And he took off like a Road Runner.

The ambulance arrived in record time. I half expected to see Popeye running along in front of it, leading the way, but he was sleeping on the patient's cot in the back.

"Hell, lieutenant," the young doctor said to Scumbag, "I expected to find a comatose patient, the way your runner described it. This man looks like he sprained his ankle."

"We thought it might be broken, Sir." The doc didn't have any rank on his whites, but Scumbag figured anyone must outrank him. "Of course the runner, the messenger, is prone to exaggeration, but then sometimes it's better to exaggerate than to ignore a possible serious casualty ..." He would have gone on philosophizing, but the doc turned his back and told his driver to supervise getting Fat Boy into the ambulance. That's when they found Popeye, and unceremoniously tossed him out of the ambulance.

We finished the march and had the next day off. Fat Boy came out of the hospital with a cast on his ankle and crutches. No break but some ligaments were torn. Company A won the regimental award for best company the whole four months we were there. They wanted to promote Captain Nugent to major, but he said no, then he'd have to go to regiment, and he thought his work as Company Commander was more important at this time of crisis for our country, so they left him alone. Lt. Scumbag complained to Captain Nugent about Sgt. Taylor, said he was insubordinate. Captain Nugent just glared at him and said, "Get the fuck out of my sight, Scumbag." He'd heard about the nickname from Sgt. Quinn. Lt. Scumbag applied for a transfer and left a week or two later. You know to where? The Pentagon in Washington, as assistant to some policy maker. No wonder the army's all fucked up.

Sgts. Taylor and Quinn and Capt. Nugent stayed at Company A to whip the next batch of trainees into shape. They decided that Sy Abrams was more valuable to the war effort as Company Clerk of A Company, so they made him a Corporal and he stayed, too. I don't know how long Sgt. Taylor stayed. He wanted to go back to Nam. Crazy bastard, but the best soldier I ever saw. Polanski was out of bed in three days and took over the medic duties again. I'd only had one patient, and Fat Boy gave me the honor of being the first to sign his cast.

3 Goodbye Vietnam

Camp Breckenridge, Kentucky, 1974

I remember the day well, because it was just after we got back from that night march. At reveille, the First Sergeant called out my name and when I raised my hand, he told me to report to him at Company HQ after chow. Because of all that marching and other strenuous stuff, we were always famished at breakfast, knowing that another similar day stood before us. So, despite being nervous, and the other guys asking me what I had done to be called to the First Sgt's fearful presence, I shoveled it down as usual. Between mouthfuls I told them I had no idea, which was true.

At HQ he told me that I had been ordered to report to Division Classification and Assignment at 9 a.m. When I asked why, he shook his head and said, "Don't know, son." I was surprised at such a benevolent expression from a tough looking guy with all those stripes and medals, not to mention a pot belly. Frankly, it worried me.

"Just go," he said. "Do you know where it is?"

"Never heard of it, Sergeant."

He told me how to get there, that I could walk it in fifteen minutes, and dismissed me with a wave of an index finger. The rest of the company had already left for the firing range and I had a couple of hours to kill. I didn't hit the sack because I was afraid I wouldn't wake up in time, so I took a paperback from my footlocker – James Jones' *From Here to Eternity* – and walked to the C&A building, then around it, then to the PX for a cup of coffee and some leisurely reading.

"Youse guys have been called here because of those IQ tests you thought were dumb that you took when you entered this man's army seemed to show that you have an aptitude for foreign languages," a sergeant told us with what smelled of a sneer, like he couldn't believe it. We were only fourteen grunts from the whole division.

"Now pay attention, cause I ain't gonna repeat it, and I only speak one language and that's army American."

Suddenly his tone and his army American changed. "According to those tests you are all qualified to attend the Army Language School in Monterey, California in order to learn one of the foreign languages the army needs or may need." He waited for that to sink in; obviously he'd done this before. "It's voluntary and there's a catch ... isn't there always?" We nodded, at least I did.

"If you decide to attend the school, and are accepted, you have to re-up – reenlist in the queen's English – for three years upon completing basic training. Is that clear?"

We were all adding up the time: after four months of basic training, another three years instead of the remaining twenty months. But we knew that we were in the pipeline to Vietnam where the war was going on and who in his right mind would prefer dodging bullets to a vacation in California? Heroes, which we weren't. No one said anything. It was clear.

He handed out applications. After filling in the usual data, we were to select our first choice of languages to be studied. They were:

Swedish

Russian

Vietnamese

Chinese

Being in one's right mind would seem to indicate that Swedish was the rational choice. Imagine spending the rest of the time after the Language School in Stockholm surrounded by beautiful Swedish broads! Vietnamese or Chinese would be for those not in their right minds. And me? I was in the midst of a Dostoevsky binge and dreamed of reading *The Brothers Karamazov* in the original, so on impulse I checked Russian, fearing that I would live to regret it.

Two weeks later we were called back to C&A. The sergeant was in a better mood. He even smiled; so did we, at first. "Bad news I'm afraid," he said. "The Swedish quota had been filled by the time your applications were received, so all your applications were rejected, except ..." he looked down at the file on his desk ... "Pvt. Marvin Jacks," who chose Russian. "Are you here, Jacks?" I raised my hand. "Answer like a fucking soldier!" he said with feigned anger, still smiling. "Yes, sergeant."

"But there's no need for the rest of you to despair. Vietnamese and Chinese are still open, so you can reapply." His eyes scanned the room. No reaction. "There's no time to consult your mothers, gentlemen, so decide right now. If you don't like those beautiful oriental languages, you can leave now." After a pause, two guys stood up and left, grumbling. The rest chose Chinese. I was in a kind of mini-shock. What did I ever do to deserve this? I asked myself. Going to sunny California to learn Russian instead of dodging gook bullets in Vietnam with winter approaching. Nothing, I decided, but it is what it is.

After basic training was over half the company was sent to Vietnam, the other half to Germany. The army decided that alphabetically: names beginning A to M to Vietnam; N to *Z* to Germany. Very scientific. I, however, was on my way to the Army Language School in Monterey, California, to study Russian for a year. That last day the whole company stood in front of the barracks in dress uniforms. First Sergeant Quinn called each man by name and handed him his orders. Then shook his hand. Field First Sergeant Silas Taylor stood next to him and shook all hands as well. The Company Commander stood a few paces behind them watching – which was correct, because he didn't really know us. I could almost swear I saw a tear in the First Sergeant's eye as he said, "Good luck, son," to each one of us.

My father drove me to the airport in New York. My duffel bag didn't fit into the trunk, so we left the trunk-lid open with the bag half out. When we got to the airport the bag wasn't there; it'd either bounced out or was stolen when we stopped for a red light. My father said he'd look for it on the way home, but it was never found. So, I arrived at the Language School with only the clothes on my back. I gradually bought the uniform stuff from quartermaster, but I didn't complain. It was better than Vietnam.

4 Обучение [Training]

Moscow, 1974

Judith Baumgartner and her future husband sat with a small group of trainees from various countries waiting to hear an introductory lecture at the Moscow Center facility. The room was spare and the chairs uncomfortable. Two men entered from the rear and took their places at a lectern. One was stocky and ferocious looking in a bulky Russian suit. The other wore a slight smile and his suit, although also of Russian make, looked as though it had been cut to fit.

"Dobrie Dyen tovarishie," the bulky one said. "Good morning, comrades," the other interpreted. And so it went, the Russian speaking first and the other interpreting with a posh British pronunciation. Judith, who understood both languages, noted that the interpretation was far from literal. Although the content was basically the same, the style was different, easier, with a few wry jokes thrown in, at which the other Russian, obviously not understanding, frowned as the audience grinned, not daring to be more demonstrative.

"You are here, comrades, in order to learn how you can best serve our Marxist-Leninist revolution. As you know, we strive to serve the working classes the world over. We are fighting for justice and equality.

Although we have been successful here in the Soviet Union thanks to our courageous leaders, and in several other countries in Eastern Europe and Africa and Central and South America, there is still much to accomplish. You have been selected by the parties in your countries as loyal, *trustworthy* socialists. I emphasize the word 'trustworthy' because trust is the most important characteristic of our work: we must trust you and you must trust us!" He paused and glared at his audience. Then he almost smiled. "I now leave you at the mercy of Comrade Kuznitsov. Good luck."

"That's me," Kuznitsov said after the bad cop had marched out. "And I *am* merciful." His smile seemed genuine, so one could almost feel the group's silent sigh of relief. Judith would eventually learn that there were no such things as mercy and mutual trust in the KGB, especially when Germans were concerned. She already knew about the lack of trust in the STASI, especially when Russians were concerned. "Your training will consist of the following ..." Several trainees took out notebooks. "No notes, please." The notebooks disappeared. "After breakfast, which is very good by the way, you are privileged to hear an indoctrination lecture. The second hour will be a course in Russian for those who do not speak it and also for those who do, who are expected to help those who do not. Also, certain technical aspects, such as interrogation techniques are included, which you may not be familiar with. I must warn you now, comrades, that failure or dropping out are not options. You already know too much for that. Even this introductory meeting is top secret."

"We, the KGB, are the world's most effective information-gathering organization. We operate – sometimes legally, sometimes illegally – in target countries where a resident – a cultural or military attaché for example – is in charge of this espionage activity. If caught – yes, it happens sometimes – he is protected by diplomatic immunity. He will then return to his own country, either voluntarily or, if declared *persona non grata* … well, he will return anyway, expelled by the target country. We then expel one of their 'diplomats,' with or without evidence. Is that fair? You may ask. Yes, because they do the same."

Now we come to the illegal comrades, those without diplomatic immunity. We have studied your files and know that most of you will be in that category. They may be prosecuted and imprisoned. Often, however, we are able to trade spies with them. If you are careful, you will not be caught."

He didn't mention those who are careful and are caught anyway because of a mole or a defector who reveals their identity. Judith knew of such a case.

"All of what I am saying also applies to your home countries, which also have diplomatic missions. The KGB and your own agencies share all the information gathered." Judith also knew that the sharing was one-sided; the KGB gets everything and the others get crumbs.

"We value the unofficial operatives more, because they are able to infiltrate more easily, whereas diplomatic personnel are suspected anyway and are followed everywhere." He glanced around the room. "Your files indicate that you all know English. I hope it's true, because this training will be in that decadent, but useful language." He smiled as though he'd just told a joke. Judith was not amused. "But I can assure you that once we have won the battle that will no longer be the case. Russian will then be the international language." No smile.

"There are several basic forms of espionage: political, economic, military-strategic, counter-intelligence and scientific-technical. We classify our spies, if I may use that loaded word, as *agents* (intelligence providers) and *controllers* (intelligence relayers). The agents have a legend, that is, a false identity. This legend is substantiated by living in a foreign country, which may or may not be the real target country, to which they will eventually immigrate with an apparently true biography. Any questions?" A young black man raised his hand. "Yes?"

"Why not go directly to the target country?" he asked in heavily accented English.

"That's a possibility, depending on your biography," Kuznitsov replied. "If the target country is the United States, for example, would you be able to obtain a permanent visa?"

"No likely," the young man said. "I communist."

"Exactly. So, you must first establish a bourgeois identity in a second country, from which you might be acceptable to the Americans. We'll go into more detail about how this works later. We will also tell you about methods of intelligence gathering, also known as spy craft, which includes stealing or photographing documents, code-names, contacts, targets, dead-letter boxes, etc."

5 The First Encounter

Monterey, California

That night I went to the Gilded Cage with a purpose and was dressed accordingly: blue sports jacket, slacks, loafers without socks, white shirt open to the third button. I arrived early and found a stool at the semi-circular bar, put a fiver on the bar for effect, ordered a Millers High Life, lit a cigarette, and looked around. The barstools were almost all occupied – by men. Soon they'd be three deep, it being Friday night. The piano was set back in an alcove to the left-rear of the bar. It also had barstools around it so you could drink there and look at the player with one elbow on the piano. Two young couples were perched on the stools, the men in suits and ties and the giggly women showing a lot of leg. The men were probably asshole officers from Fort Ord, I figured. The piano player was playing *As Time Goes By*, probably requested by one of the girls. That kind of girl always requested that kind of song because they liked to think of themselves as Ingrid Bergman – romantic and teary – without realizing that it wasn't a song you could request, it had to hit you out of the blue. I lit another cigarette and nursed my beer.

The Gilded Cage wasn't really my kind of place, primarily because they only served bottled beer which cost two bits, except for Miller's

High Life, which went for thirty cents. Hell, you could get a good glass of draft anywhere else for a dime. There were other things I didn't like about it, such as the yellow birdcage hanging over the bar with a live parakeet in it and the bartender wearing a tie and garters on his sleeves. I wondered what it felt like to be a caged bird in that dump. The whole place was like a trinket you could buy in the five-and-ten. And the customers – mostly what you'd call gay today but what we called something else then – thought they were hot shit with their sports jackets and ties and wavy hair and loud laughs. About the only thing good about the Gilded Cage was the piano player, who could play anything you asked for. You had to tip him or buy him a drink every time you made a request though, so I never requested anything because I was only a private in the United States Army and my budget didn't include tips, except to waitresses. In fact, I'd only been in the Gilded Cage once before, on a payday, when I wandered in drunk without knowing what kind of place it was. Monterey was full of cheap bars and the only reason to go to an expensive one would be on the chance of picking up a girl, which was damn hard in a town that had the Army Language School right up the hill in the Presidium and Fort Ord about five miles away. Monterey wasn't Steinbeck's Cannery Row anymore, and it hadn't yet become a snooty extension of Carmel and Pacific Grove. It wasn't much of anything, as far as I was concerned.

"Nice song," a guy said who sidled up next to me. I nodded and looked at him in the mirror. In his thirties, I guessed, suntanned, casually well dressed. He was smiling at my profile. "And from a nice picture," I agreed.

"Saw it three times myself," the guy said. "You?"

"About the same."

"You want your drink here, Jacky?" the bartender asked the guy.

"Yes, thank you, Sal." The bartender went to the end of the bar and came back with a glass with an inch of whiskey and soda in it. He put a coaster in front of Jacky and placed the drink on it. "That was hardly worth the trip, Sal," Jacky said, grinning. Sal grinned back and went off to tend a customer. I drank down my beer, knowing I wouldn't have to nurse it any longer. Jacky drank his down too. "Let me buy you a drink. Wouldn't you prefer scotch?"

"No, I'll stick to Millers thanks." A subtle answer, so Jacky wouldn't get the right idea.

"Suit yourself," he said. "Sal, another scotch for me and a Millers for … What did you say your name was?"

"Marvin."

"For Marvin," Jacky said smoothly, more to me than to the bartender, who had moved on anyway.

"Thanks."

"Cigarette?" He held a pack of filter-tipped Parliaments, though my Marlboro's were plainly visible on the bar. What the hell, I decided, why waste them? and took a Parliament. Jacky's gold-plated lighter flicked open under my nose so I didn't even have to lean forward to reach the tiny flame. I dragged and could hardly taste the smoke. Goddam filter-tips!

"Thanks."

"Are you from around here, Marvin?"

"No, New York." Actually Brooklyn, but that always caused a laugh or some wise guy remark, so I had learned to say New York instead. Hell, most people west of New Jersey didn't even know that Brooklyn was in New York City.

"You don't sound like you're from New York."

One thing good about learning a foreign language was that you had to concentrate on your pronunciation and I had begun to watch my English as well to weed out the Brooklynese.

"Well, I am."

"In the army here?"

"Yeah."

"Fort Ord?"

"Language School."

"Thank God!"

I looked at him. "Why?"

"Well, you know," Jacky said smiling, "you can at least have an intelligent conversation with a Language School student, which isn't often the case with the ones from Fort Ord. You're an officer, I suppose."

"Why do you suppose that? Officers are assholes."

He laughed loudly. "Marvin, you're a man after my own heart, and you're absolutely right. Officers are assholes."

I glanced at the couples at the piano, but they obviously couldn't hear. "So why did you suppose I was one?"

"Oh god, please don't be angry. I just wanted to know and I couldn't very well have said: You're a private, I suppose? I mean what if you were an officer. Where would I be then?"

"Up shit's creek?" I laughed as I said it.

"Absolutely."

"Not many officers in the Language School," I said. I liked the game of denigrating officers, but kept my voice low. "They're too dumb."

"I agree, absolutely, at least the few I've met."

I didn't say anything. I was waiting for the proposition.

"What language are you studying?" Jacky asked.

"Russian."

"Russian? Wow, that must be difficult."

"Yeah, but it's better than Chinese."

"Oh God, yes. I speak some French myself, but I'd never think of trying a difficult language like Russian. Whatever made you pick it?"

"I didn't have much choice. They called a few of us to Classification and Assignment one day in Basic Training and said that the tests showed we had linguistic abilities and offered a choice between Swedish, Russian and Chinese Mandarin, we should write down our preference. I put Russian because I'd like to be able to read Dostoyevsky and Tolstoy in the original. So, I got it – Russian I mean. The others all put down Swedish and none of them got anything. They're in Vietnam now."

"I love Dostoyevsky," Jacky crooned.

"Yeah, well I'm still far away from being able to read him in Russian, the way the course is going, prisoner interrogation exercises, that kind of shit."

"How long have you been here?"

"Two months."

"So, you have ten months left?"

So, Jacky knew that Russian was a year-long course. Well, why not? He was from around here.

"That's right."

"Wonderful!" He patted the back of my hand. "We have time to get acquainted."

"Here it comes," I thought. "Yeah, but I doubt if there's time to learn enough Russian to read Dostoyevsky or Tolstoy in the original. They're tough."

"Would you be very disappointed if you couldn't, Marvin?"

"Not very, but disappointed, sure, I guess."

"I think it's a question of what one expects from life. If one has no expectations one can't be disappointed. Don't you think so?"

"Well, I think life would be pretty boring without expectations."

"But not disappointing."

"I don't know about that."

"Have you ever been disappointed, Marvin," Jacky asked and laughed. "I don't know where you find room for all that beer. Sal, another round, please."

"You're keeping up with me."

"Yes, but there's less liquid involved."

"More potent liquid though ... and yes, I have."

"Have what, Marvin?"

"Yes, I have been disappointed."

"But you're so young to have been disappointed, unless in love." He smiled. Actually he was a handsome guy. "But then Romeo was awfully young. Have you been disappointed in love then, Marvin? I have. Often."

"Yeah, especially the last time," I said, wondering why I was about to tell him about Olga when I hadn't mentioned her to anyone else, not even my buddies up at the Presidium. I was too young to know that we are always on the lookout for a sympathetic listener. And Jacky was certainly one, while my buddies would only have shook their heads and laughed.

"Oh, do tell me." Jacky leaned to his left until our shoulders were touching and looked at me intently, ready to listen.

"Well, I went up to San Francisco." I didn't mention that it had been last weekend. I had driven up alone in my 1949 Hudson Hornet the Friday after payday, alone because I'm a loner, that's what people say about me and I suppose it's true. I had only one real friend on the hill in the Language School, Jim McCrea, but Jim was black which was a big disadvantage when girls were involved. In fact it was a disadvantage when anything was involved once you got off base. There was no Jim Crow in California like in the South, but there was a more subtle discrimination. Jim and I had driven around sightseeing and had eaten together in restaurants and went to Shorty's bar, which was just outside the base, at least once a week to drink ten cent beer and listen to jazz on the jukebox they had there and talk a lot. But whenever there were likely looking girls in the place, which wasn't often, I regretted being with Jim because it was impossible to pick up a couple of white girls – and they were always in pairs – if you were with Jim. Even if you went to town, like tonight, you might get into trouble if some townie or redneck from Fort Ord decided to pick a fight because Jim was black. Jim knew it, of course, so he never went to the bars in town. I had to do that. It was a rotten situation that I hated, but if you were after pussy that was how it was and if I had to choose between pussy – or the chance of it – and Jim ... well, that's the way it was.

It took about three hours to get to Frisco because there was no good thruway yet. Once there, I checked into the YMCA for three bucks a night that I paid in advance and went cruising. I had consumed a lot of beer by the time I walked into that bar without noticing its name – an oversight I would eternally regret.

It was about midnight and the place was jumping. There was a rectangular bar, served by two bartenders on all fours sides, a crowded dance floor and booths. The first unusual thing was that there was a dance floor at all, the second that the place was well lighted instead of half dark. It was the antithesis of the Gilded Cage. I stood at the bar and ordered a Bud draft. The booths ran all along the walls and I inspected them. There were a lot of girls in the place but they were already with guys. I regretted that I hadn't found the place sooner. Now I'd have to try to cut someone out or wait for someone new to come in.

Then I spotted Olga. Although there must have been a lot of servicemen there – we were in the middle of the Vietnam War after all – none were in uniform except the sailor in a funny uniform who was sitting in the booth across from her. The sailor moved his hand brusquely and knocked over a wine bottle. The girl tried to wipe the spilled wine with a paper napkin while he laughed. He must have been drunk. I saw my opportunity and grabbed a rag from the sink below the bar and walked over to them. "You won't get it dry with that piece of paper, Miss," I said, and wiped up the beer. The sailor clapped me on the shoulder laughing and said something in French.

"What'd he say?" I asked her.

"He thinks you're a waiter. He asked for another bottle of wine." She smiled at me and I smiled back. She had an accent which I thought I recognized, having heard it often enough during the past two months.

"He looks like he's had enough," I said. "But hey, I'm not a waiter, so don't ask me."

The Frenchy suddenly keeled over on his side.

"What'd I tell you?" I pushed him upright and sat down next to him across from the girl and the sailor slumped against me. "You're Russian, aren't you?"

"Does it show so much?"

I looked her over carefully as if to decide whether it showed. Her cheekbones were a little high, eyes set wide apart, full lips. Her brown hair flowed over her shoulders front and back with ragged bangs on her forehead. She was wearing a greenish print dress that looked like it came straight out of a World War II Care package. Her bosom was full, apparent, although the dress was buttoned up almost to her neck, to anyone who looked, and I was looking. No makeup. Pretty. She looked very young at first glance, but her eyes were older.

"No," I said, "I recognize the accent."

"Most people think I'm Polish. How did you guess I'm Russian?"

"That's because there's so many Poles around and not many Russians," I said. "I recognized the accent because I'm around Russians all the time. I'm studying Russian at the Army Language School. *Ya izuchayu russkie Yazuik f'armeskiye shkole Yizikom.*"

At that she clapped her hands happily and let out a stream of Russian of which I only caught a few words.

"Hey, wait a minute, I've only been at it a couple of months."

She repeated it slowly and, though I still didn't understand everything, I got the drift: "How wonderful. The only people I know here who speak Russian are Russians, and they bore me."

"Do I bore you?"

"Of course not. That's what I meant." We both smiled. The juke box started to play *As Time Goes By* and I tried to think of the word for dance in Russian and finally decided that I never knew it.

"Would you like to dance?"

"*Konyechno.*"

I pushed the sailor away until he was leaning against the wall, but not until after his head bounced against it.

"Be careful!" she cried.

"Don't worry," I said as we walked to the dance floor, "he can feel no pain. Where did you ever find that guy?"

"He's a friend of my uncle's who lives in Paris. Actually he's the son of my uncle's friend." She looked back at the sailor. "His ship sails at dawn and he has to get back somehow."

We began a bit stiffly, but she was soon snuggling up against me and I could smell the delicate perfume of her hair. I pulled my crotch back so she wouldn't feel my incipient erection, not yet anyway. I had already drunk enough beer to feel light-headed.

"*Kak vasho imyo?*" I asked, the easiest question there was.

She laughed though.

"What's so funny?"

"You're so formal. My name is Olga, but you would normally use the familiar form of the pronoun under the present circumstances: *Kak tvayo imyo?*"

"We haven't had the familiar form yet."

"Well, we can't very well continue as if I were your professor, so we better speak English."

"Excellent idea, Olga. I love your name."

"Oh dear, and it's such a common name in Russia."

"Not here. Here it's beautiful – to me at least."

"And your name?" she asked leaning back to look in my eyes, which caused her hips to swivel into me.

"Marvin." My erection was in full bloom. I moved back so it was only touching her lightly.

"You don't have to do that," she said. "I like it."

Godamm, my dream had been answered, my ship had come in. I was on the verge of shacking up in Frisco with a beautiful Russian woman, who not only liked erections and wasn't afraid to say so, but could help me learn Russian.

A Chubby Checker teenybop number blasted out of the jukebox and Olga said she didn't like it so we went to the bar instead of back to the booth, where Frenchy was still out cold. She didn't want anything more to drink though, said she already had too much wine. I ordered a beer, drank it down and ordered another. I had worked up a real thirst from dancing and the expectation of what was to come – that night and many future weekends.

Olga took a sip of my beer. "I don't think that Philippe is in any condition to get back to his ship," she said, frowning.

"He's only asleep," I said. "He'll be all right."

"I hope so." She looked at her watch. "It's almost two o'clock."

"Good. This place will be open another hour. Let's dance." The divine Sarah Vaughan was singing *A Foggy Day*. She meant in London town, but San Francisco town was pretty foggy too.

"I don't know how he'll get back to his ship."

"After this number we'll go back, wake him up and put him in a cab," I said, hoping that either the sailor or she had money to pay for it.

"Oh no, we couldn't do that."

"He's probably got money, sailors always do after hoarding it up at sea."

"That's just it," she protested. "You know what taxi drivers are like. A drunk sailor. He'd be robbed ... "

"Rolled," I corrected her. "Not necessarily. All cabbies aren't crooks. Why are you worrying about him so much anyway?" I didn't want to sound jealous, but I was.

"Don't you see? I'm responsible for him. They gave him my name in Paris because they knew he was coming here. He called me – he's very nice when he's sober – and I took him out to see San Francisco. He had too much to drink. If anything happens to him I'd be responsible. Do you see?"

"Yeah, I guess so."

"You have a car, Marvin. Could you take him?"

"Well, I don't know," though I did know: I couldn't refuse her. "Where's his ship at?"

"He said it was at l'ille du tresor. Was it a joke?"

"No, that would be Treasure Island, it's a naval base under the Bay Bridge to Oakland."

"So, you know it!"

"I passed it a couple of times going over the bridge, that's all. I saw the sign."

"Will you take him, Marvin, please?"

"O.K., we'll all go." I tried to push her into dance mode again, but she stood still.

"No, I'm a foreigner, they wouldn't let me in. And.. well ... my papers aren't completely in order yet."

Shit. Was she a spy? Were they both spies? Who cares.

"But you're in the military. They'd let you in. I'll wait here for you."

"What if this place is closed when I get back? You can't stand waiting on the corner at three o'clock in the morning."

Her eyes opened wide; they were green like her dress. "I'll give you my telephone number. If it's closed when you get back, call me." She smiled. "I'll be waiting."

My first priority had been to go to her place when the bar closed. Failing that, I wanted her phone number. I wasn't sure that she'd give it to me. After all, I was only a barroom pick up. Now, however, I was sure of getting it, and I couldn't refuse her anyway. "Okay," I said, "let's get it over with."

We went back to the booth and I shook Frenchy and slapped his cheeks. He woke up and babbled in French.

Olga took one of the paper napkins from its holder and wrote her telephone number on it. I put it in my pocket, I couldn't remember which one afterwards, although I certainly thought about it a lot.

"C'mon Robespierre, let's get you presentable." I pulled him across the booth seat and got him standing.

"What are you doing?" Olga asked.

"Taking him to the john to put some cold water on his face and get him to take a leak or he'll piss all over the car."

"Jesus, I never saw anyone so drunk from wine," I said as we maneuvered him out of the bar upon our return from the men's room. "Refused to piss, that's his problem."

"He was a little tipsy when he came to my place," Olga said, sounding as though she was defending him. "Who knows how much he had to drink."

My car was a block away and as the three of us weaved downhill the sailor started singing – in French of course.

"Christ, Just what I needed," I said. "Tell him to shut up before the MPs hear him, or SPs if that'll impress him more."

He shut up quick when Olga translated. We dumped him in the front seat of the Hudson and Olga kissed me on the lips, not passionately, but lovingly yes, I decided.

I took some wrong turns so it took longer to find the Bay Bridge than I'd expected. The fog had gotten worse so I had to drive more carefully than usual. I remembered that the sign to Treasure Island was somewhere near the middle of the bridge, so I hugged the right lane in order not to miss the turn-off, which was on the bridge itself. The fog was even thicker on the bridge and I drove slowly, for me, hunched over the steering wheel. Then I felt the car descending and had a sinking feeling in my stomach. I had missed the exit to Treasure Island. And I couldn't very well make a U-turn on a bridge when I couldn't see what might be coming from the other direction. So, I had to continue into Oakland, turn and go back over the bridge. I knew there was only one turn-off and it was on the right side going towards Oakland. So, I had to drive all the way back into Frisco, turn and head back to Oakland.

This time I went ten miles an hour and finally saw the sign: it was hanging over the middle of the bridge, that's why I hadn't seen it the first time across. They must have moved it. I cursed and eased the Hudson down the ramp onto Treasure Island and stopped at the guard booth.

"Where ya goin, sir," a huge SP said. The "sir" was just in case I was an officer.

"I'm trying to get this French sailor back to his ship," I said, trying to sound like one.

"Uh huh. ID, please."

I showed him my ID, which definitely established my non-officer status.

"Where ya stationed, soldier?" the SP asked.

"Army Language School, Monterey."

"What's the matter wit ya friend?"

I looked over at the sailor, who had fallen asleep again. "He had one too many, I guess." I gave him a jab in the chest with my elbow to wake him up. "He's French."

"Yeah, I had a bunch of 'em rollin in tonight. What about you?"

"No sweat, I'm okay."

"You better be. I keep your ID and you can pick it up when you leave." He noted down the Hudson's license plate number on a chart and went back into his booth.

"Hey," I yelled.

"Waddya want?"

"Can you tell me where the French ship is?"

The SP checked a chart hanging in the booth and said: "Pier 21. Go straight till ya can't no more, turn right till ya can't no more, then right again and that's it. Got a French flag on it I guess."

"What's a French flag look like?"

"How the fuck should I know."

I followed the SP's instructions and found the ship. An armed French sailor on guard duty was standing at the foot of the gangplank. I looked at my watch: three o'clock. Shit, the bar was closing. What's it called? "Hey, Frenchy," I said to the sailor, "what's the name of that bar we were in?"

He looked at me blankly.

"Comment lapel le bar?" No reaction.

"Hey," I called to the guard, "come and get this asshole." He didn't move. I got out, opened the door and dragged Frenchy out. Then I grabbed the hat with the red pom from the seat and placed it on his head and pushed him at the sailor, who had no choice but to catch him.

"Adieu, shitheads."

I parked on a deserted street in San Francisco and looked through my pockets for the napkin. It wasn't there. I looked desperately, turning my pockets out. Then I took a flashlight from the glove compartment and searched the car – floor, seats, everywhere. No napkin.

"Can we help you, sir?" one of the two MPs who appeared behind me said.

"No, I was just looking for sumpin." Damn it, I wasn't drunk anymore, why was I slurring my speech.

"You in the service?"

"Yeah. Who isn't?" Wise guy answers, just what MPs like to hear.

"Let's see your ID."

Here we go again.

Finally, they let me go but made me leave my car where it was, claiming I was drunk, and told me to go right back to the Y and if they saw me again that night, I'd spend the rest of it in the clink.

All day Sunday I searched for the bar where I had found and lost Olga but didn't find it. It was as if it had vanished into thin air or never really existed. At three o'clock in the morning I drove back to Monterey, not too drunk but enough to be picked up, so I drove carefully. I had to be in class at seven and sick calls on Monday mornings were frowned upon.

"Marvin," Jacky said with a crooked smile, "I can imagine how you felt – and I'm sorry, truly I am."

My glass was empty, and I called Sal without bothering to wait for Jacky to invite me to have another.

"On the other hand, I think it goes to prove my thesis."

"Oh yeah? How's that?"

"Well, if you hadn't had the expectation that you'd found the perfect shack job who would help you with Russian as well, you wouldn't have been disappointed when she didn't materialize. See what I mean?"

"Yeah, I guess so." But it was more than that. I had fallen head over heels in love with Olga and I needed to find her. No need to tell Jackie that though.

As Time Goes By was being played again.

"God, I'm beginning to hate that song," Jacky said.

"Me too." I hadn't mentioned the detail that that was the song Olga and I had first danced to.

"What kind of music do you like, Marvin, I mean really like?"

"Oh you know, Jazz, blues. Sarah Vaughan knocks me out, but I guess she's not coming in here."

"My God, Marvin, I knew we were kindred spirits," Jacky gushed. "Listen, I have an idea."

Here it comes, finally.

"Let's go to my place. I have the most fantastic jazz collection you ever heard, including plenty of Sarah Vaughan, before she went commercial."

"I like her commercial too."

"Well so do I, but the non-commercial stuff is better, believe me. How about it?"

"Where do you live?"

"Carmel." Exactly where I had guessed he lived.

"Oh, no then, I couldn't go there."

"Why in heaven's name not?"

"No gas. I'll be lucky to get back to the Presidium."

Jacky laughed, obviously much relieved. "No problem my dear friend, we'll go in my car and I'll bring you back later, if you like, or tomorrow. I have plenty of room."

"Naw, I always like to have my own wheels," I intoned, smoking calmly. "Thanks anyway."

Jacky laughed again. "Marvin, you're amazing. You make problems out of nothing. Come on, let's get gas for your car, silly."

"I'm afraid I'm sort of broke, Jacky," I said, although there were still four dollars and seventy cents in front of me on the bar.

"I had no intention of letting you pay for it even if you had the money. When you're my guest it means in everything." He clapped me on the shoulder. "Sal, my bill, please!"

I only needed about a dollar's worth of gas to get to Carmel and back, but I told the attendant at the service station to fill it up. I looked at my watch: ten o'clock, plenty of time. Jacky had pulled his white Mercedes into the station away from the pumps and stood waiting with his arms folded and a big grin on his face. When the attendant hung up the gas hose he strolled over and paid for my gas.

"Follow me, okay Marvin? Can't lose that car." He put his wallet in his pocket and started back to his Mercedes whistling *As Time Goes By*, realized it and stopped.

"Jacky," I called.

"Yes, Marvin?" He turned around and came back. "What is it?"

"I'm not going to your place, Jacky, it was just a con. I needed the gas to get to Frisco, see? To look for Olga."

Jacky was openly crestfallen, but he didn't beg, I have to give him that. "I see," he said, looking at the ground. Actually, I kind of felt sorry for him. He was a nice guy, basically – but he wasn't Olga.

I got back into the Hudson, closed the door and said through the open window as I started the engine: "You shouldn't have expectations, Jacky, and you wouldn't be disappointed." I didn't mean it sarcastically, although it came out that way.

I closed the window against the cold drizzle, turned on the windshield wipers and gunned the Hudson Hornet towards San Francisco where I, at least, still had expectations. I should have listened to my own advice though, for I never found Olga there.

6 Camp King

Oberursel, West Germany

Second Lt. Marvin Jacks tied his sneaker shoelaces and stood up. He heard basketball sounds coming from the gym: hard bounces on a wooden floor, the clang when the ball hit the rim, a whumpf when it went through cleanly. Shouts of triumph or despair. He looked at himself in the locker-room mirror and smiled with satisfaction. Smiling back at him was a young handsome face, the only imperfection on it being a slightly bent nose broken in a street fight during adolescence. He'd never had it straightened because it provided the manly touch his baby-face needed if he was to be taken seriously. He was only slightly above average height, too small for basketball, at least for the professional sort.

He opened the door to the gym and was surprised to see one person, playing by himself, in the act of sinking a jump shot. He retrieved the ball and said "Hi" to Jacks.

"Hi. I thought there'd be two complete teams in here, judging by the noise," Jacks said with a smile.

"Yeah. I like to make it realistic. No fun otherwise." He trotted over and offered his hand. He was about Jacks' height but heavier. "Jack Quinn. You're new, I guess."

"Marvin Jacks. Yeah, just got in."

"Welcome to Spook's Paradise." He flipped the ball to Jacks and stationed himself under the basket. Jacks was conscious of the dramatic effect a basket on first try would make. He bounced the ball twice, drifted to the center of the court and let loose a long jumper that bounced vertically off the rim, touched the backboard and went in.

"Good shot."

"Lucky."

"Same difference."

They spent the next fifteen minutes dribbling, passing behind their backs and shooting with uncanny accuracy. An observer would have thought they'd been playing together for years.

"You from New York?" Jacks asked, knowing he was because the accent was unmistakable.

"Sure. You too, I bet."

"Brooklyn."

"No kidding. What part?"

"Flatbush. What other part is there?"

"Bensonhurst, that's what other part."

"You play good ball," Jacks said as he missed a jumper. "Who'd you play for?"

"Playground ball. You?"

"Erasmus High."

"Good teams." Quinn drove in, feinted at nobody, glided under the basket and sunk a twisting left-hander. He retrieved the ball and placed it under his arm, a gesture that indicated that the conversation would get serious. "Play any baseball, Marvin?"

"A little, nothing to speak of."

"That's OK, you're a good athlete. I can shape you up."

"What do you mean?" Jacks asked, wiping the sweat off his face with his arm.

"I mean this here's an M.I. unit," Quinn said, "but it's also a jockstrap outfit."

"No kidding?"

"Sure. The old man's a sports nut, played for Georgia Tech. Don't see how myself. His best, let's say his only shot, is a hooker. I mean Jesus, that went out with Ebbets Field."

"Unless you happen to be seven feet tall."

"Which he ain't. Comes in to work out most every day when he's here." As if to emphasize what he would say next, Quinn dribbled the ball between his legs, gave it a kick-flip with his toe and caught it. "What I'm saying, Marvin, is that you could spend your whole tour right here in Camp King just playing basketball and baseball. No football, not enough jocks and anyway the equipment's too expensive." He sighed at that misfortune. "It's a great place, food's fantastic, Frankfurt's a half-hour away on the trolley, nothing to do but play ball."

"Nothing?"

"A little interrogating if you don't object. Basketball in the fall and winter, baseball in the spring and summer. That's all. We're in the service units league. Bunch of beer-bellies. We win everything. Just say the word. I coach both teams."

The locker-room door opened and a man walked onto the floor in gym clothes. "Hey, I thought no one was here. Didn't hear anything."

"Howya doin' sir? We were just takin' a break," Quinn said.

"Who are you?" he asked Marvin.

"Jacks, sir. Arrived today."

"Oh yeah." He stood in the key and Quinn passed him the ball as he moved to his left. He hooked it high off the backboard into the basket.

"Good shot," Quinn cried. "Sure haven't lost the old touch."

Colonel Moultrie Banks, Commanding Officer of the 509th M.I. Unit, wasn't exactly as old as the hills. He was forty-five, tall and once lanky, red-nosed and high-voiced and came from Moultrie, Georgia, which one of his ancestors founded during the eighteenth century. The three of them tossed the ball around a while, until Banks began to huff and puff and the sweat poured off him in streams.

"See you guys," he said and disappeared into the locker-room.

"See what I mean?" Quinn winked. "Think about it and let me know. What barracks are you in?"

"BOQ," Jacks said. From the look of surprise on Quinn's face, it was obvious he hadn't known that Jacks was an officer. He knew exactly what Jack Quinn was thinking because he'd have been thinking it himself if the roles had been reversed: Why didn't you tell me you were a fucking officer? But all Quinn said was "Oh." Then, "See ya," and he went into the locker-room leaving Marvin Jacks alone feeling like a traitor, which in a sense he was.

When the Vietnam War broke out he had already been influenced by the romanticism of books like *From Here To Eternity* and movies like *Paths of Glory*, which depicted officers as an arrogant, selfish, privileged class of incompetent parasites who did not hesitate to send soldiers to certain death for no purpose other than their own aggrandizement.

What changed in the Language School at Monterey was his perception of moral necessity. While his comrades from basic training were being killed and wounded in Vietnam he had become one of the privileged ones – still a Private, true, but in a university atmosphere getting an education for which he was being paid. Most of the students were enlisted men, but the few officers were enveloped by enhanced privilege. They were paid much more, had new or nearly new cars and were treated almost as equals by the aristocratic staff of Russian teachers, who invited them to their homes, something a mere soldier could never attain to.

Marvin saw all this, but combined with resentment he felt envy. He began to like army life. He was part of a great family, the members of which were fed, clothed, housed and paid without having to work. The possibility of being wounded or killed in a war was always present of course, but he had been able to avoid that so far.

Halfway through his one-year Russian course he applied for OCS. Again, to his surprise he was accepted and attended the Officers Candidate School at Fort Benning, Georgia after Language School, for six months, still not long enough for the war in Vietnam to have ended. But there was still the Cold War. So, he was sent off to Germany and still another school, the Intelligence and Military Police School in Oberammergau, Bavaria, where he was supposed to learn how to be a spy. It was only a three-week course and amateurish. The only thing he remembered from it was how to conduct surveillance and a two-day long course in German history, given by a Master Sergeant who really knew his stuff. Jacks wondered what the hell he was doing in the army, and as an Enlisted Man. He could have become an officer but probably didn't want to, for which Jacks admired him more than for his historical erudition.

7 Camp King (cont.)

Lieutenant Jacks reported to his Commanding Officer, Colonel G. Moultrie Banks, on the day after his arrival at Camp King.

"Just get in, Lieutenant?" Banks asked, reading his personal file.

"Yesterday, sir. We sort of met at the gym yesterday."

He looked up at Jacks and frowned. "Oh yes. I thought you were a friend of Quinn's."

"No, sir. Never saw him before."

"Good ball player, Quinn."

"Yes, sir."

"Sit down." Jacks sat down. "You're pretty good yourself."

"I could say the same for you, sir." It was the right thing to say. In fact, if Marvin hadn't used exactly those words at exactly that time and in that place and in that admiring but matter-of-fact manner, his whole life might have been different.

The Colonel smiled modestly. "Oh, I used to be pretty good, had a great hook shot if I do say so myself." He entered into a long account of his basketball prowess at Georgia Tech. "I don't regret turning down that pro offer because that's about when the really big guys came along and my hook-shot wouldn't't've stood a snowball's chance in hell against them."

Marvin didn't dispute it. He waited.

Banks looked down again at his file. "My problem now is what the hell to do with you, Jacks."

"Sir?"

"I see you're a Russian linguist. Three fluents."

"Yes, sir."

"Do you have any suggestions as to what we're supposed to do with another Russian linguist around here?"

"Well ... no, sir."

"Of course you don't. Are you expecting a war with Russia any time soon?"

"Not really."

"Neither am I. Of course we've got the shit squad, but there's already a Major and two Captains there who do nothing and three naturalized Russian Enlisted Men who do the work."

"The shit squad, sir?" Jacks asked, worried.

"We got spies who steal the garbage from the Russian garrisons in East Germany and send the papers to us by the truckload. And the Russians use anything they can get to wipe their asses with ... get the point? But at least it's dry shit. So, our shit squad reviews these ... documents, we call them ... for potential intelligence data. Ninety-nine per cent of it is shit, love letters, pleas to Mom to send food, and so forth. Every once in a great while something of remote intelligence value is found. Get the point?"

"Yes, sir," Marvin replied, more worried.

"Is that what you'd like to do?"

"Not really, sir." A spark of hope. Was he being given a choice?

"Would you like to infiltrate the Soviet Union?"

"Well, I speak fluent Russian, but I don't think I'd pass for a Russian. No, I don't think there'd be much point in that, sir." Worried again, very worried.

"No. But they keep sending me Russian linguists. Get the point?"

"Yes, sir."

"Do you know what I need?"

"German linguists, sir?"

"Right, by God." He lit a cigarette and offered one to Marvin, who accepted it. "I knew you had a head on your shoulders. Do you know why?"

"I'd rather pass on that one, sir, as I don't know much about the operation yet. Except to say that we are in Germany, after all."

Banks grinned. "It's really obvious, isn't it? This here's an interrogation center. We get a Russian once in a blue moon and we get to keep him about two days before the CIA comes and grabs him. But we get loads of Germans: Volkspolizei, politicians, spies, double agents, phonies, the works. So, they send me Russian linguists. I get some Germans, linguists I mean, but most aren't up to the job. Do you know why?"

"No, sir."

"No balls." He waited for a reaction, but Jacks was impassive, feeling that was the appropriate stance for someone with balls. "They can be interrogators, but do you know what I really need?"

Jacks could tell that the Colonel was an experienced interrogator. "No, sir."

"Recruiters. Do you know what they do?"

"More or less. They mentioned the subject in Oberammergau."

"Yeah. Well, you gotta be able to drink beer and talk soccer to Germans to gain their confidence. Do you do those things?"

"Yes, sir," which was half a lie. He drank beer, who doesn't? But talk soccer, who does?

"Goddamn," Colonel Banks exclaimed. "You play soccer?"

"Used to. Not too much, but I could hold my own."

"Where?"

"High school." A lie, he'd never played soccer in his life and didn't know the first thing about it. He resolved to get a book on the game first thing if he got out of this interview without the Colonel asking technical questions and finding him out.

"Well, waddaya know. Can't stand the thing myself. Sorta sissy game, don't you think?"

"Not really, sir. Of course it's not football, but it can be rough and you have to be in good shape." Couldn't be anything wrong in that, he thought.

Colonel Banks sighed. "I guess you're right. The Germans aren't exactly pansies and they go for it big."

Jacks nodded wisely.

"You'd make a good recruiter, Jacks, but you don't speak German, do you?"

"As a matter of fact I do, sir."

Banks opened his eyes wide. "You do? Where'd you learn German?"

"From my mother. She was German."

"Well, I'll be dollgarned. Read and write it too?"

"Not as well as speaking. But yes, though I make mistakes writing."

"Who the hell doesn't? How come that's not in your records?"

"Don't know, sir. I guess because they never asked."

"Son, you have come to the right place. What do you know about interrogation?"

"What they taught us in Russian at the Language School. I guess the technique's the same for German."

"Yes, well, what they taught you and the reality aren't exactly the same. But practice makes perfect, just like in basketball.

"Right, sir."

"You can observe interrogations for a while, then do some easy ones on your own. Meantime tell Quinn to set you up for the basketball team. Play baseball too?"

"Some, Sir."

"OK, glad to have you aboard, Jacks."

"That's good of you, sir." He was saying all the right things, he realized. Robert E. Pruitt of *From Here to Eternity* would act differently. Well, you have to watch your own ass in the real world.

8 The Officer's Club

Marvin Jacks was ebullient. He went to the Officers' Club because he was passing it and was thirsty after that throat-drying interview with Col. Moultrie Banks. It had been the German Officers' Club before the Americans took it over and it was opulent. Marvin passed an empty reading room and entered the bar. There was only one early bird in civilian clothes perched on a bar stool reading Stars and Stripes. Marvin did a double take: it was Jack Quinn. So, he was an officer after all. What had made Marvin discount that possibility? Something straight, honest, unhypocritical about him? He was relieved and at the same time somehow disappointed. He approached smiling and said, "Hi, Jack." Quinn turned his head sideways, saw who it was, said "Hi," and resumed reading. A brush off.

"How's everything, Jack?"

Quinn looked at him stonily. "Look, top grade enlisted men can use the officers' club on this base, which I don't normally do. I'm waiting for Colonel Banks, who wants to talk to me about the sports program and this is his favorite place. That's just in case you're wondering what I'm doing here or in case you might confuse me with an officer."

Marvin ordered a beer and tried to think of what to say. It would be stupid to apologize, he had nothing to apologize for, rather it was Quinn who was being rude. Better be matter-of-fact.

"What rank are you, anyway?"

Without looking up from his paper, Quinn answered, "Master Sergeant."

That's who he reminded him of: the Master Sergeant Burt Lancaster played in *From Here To Eternity*. He despised officers, too. "You're pretty young to be a Master Sergeant," Marvin said.

Quinn sighed and closed the paper in a show of resignation. "Thank Vietnam," he said, "in case you've heard of it. Rank comes fast there if you stay long enough."

"How long were you there?"

"Long enough." Then, to the German barman, "*Noch ein Bier, Hans, bitte.*"

"Do you speak German?"

"Everyone learns to order another beer after three days here. But as a matter of fact I do. That's why I'm in this outfit."

"Language school?"

"No, my old lady."

"German speakers being in such short supply," Jacks said, "I'm surprised you aren't employed differently."

"I told you, Colonel Banks is a sports nut. Look, Jacks, I shot off my mouth yesterday about all that thinking you were ... not knowing what you were. I'd appreciate your keeping it to yourself."

He talks to me as though he were the colonel, Marvin thought, but that's the way Master Sergeants are. "No problem," he said. "By the way, Colonel Banks told me to tell you to set me up for the basketball team."

"Wow, good for you. You must have made a big hit with the old man. And it takes an expert ass-kisser to do that." Nasty.

"You seem to be pretty good at it yourself," Marvin retorted, giving up the attempt to be friendly, let alone make friends.

But he didn't know Jack Quinn, who frowned, then grinned. "The only genuine, successful ass-kissers in this man's army are officers, of which select group you are one. But maybe you're different. After all, you *are* from Brooklyn, so you can't be all bad."

Colonel Banks clapped Quinn on the shoulder. "Hello, Jack." He ignored Marvin Jacks.

"Hi, Colonel," Quinn greeted him. Marvin picked up his beer, mumbled an apology and slunk off. They didn't hear him.

9 Second Encounter

"Are you comfortable in your quarters, Frau Cornelius?" Lt. Jacks asked the attractive young lady seated across from him in Bavarian-American accented German. It was his first interrogation on his own, but he had been advised that it was routine, she was merely a defector's wife. The room was small but tastefully decorated and they sat in padded chairs. During the war the Germans had used it for the good-cop part of interrogation. If the P.O.W.s, American and British flyers, were not cooperative they went next to the dungeon below for a few days for bad-cop softening up, no torture, just isolation, were then brought back up for more officer and gentleman treatment. Most stuck to the name, rank and serial number bit, but some were willing to discuss personal things like wives, children, home towns, with their interrogators, and this inevitably led to elements of military information. Either way, they all wound up in P.O.W. camps.

The East Germans the Americans questioned were told they were there voluntarily and were free to go at any time – which was partly true: they could leave, but if they didn't return within twenty-four hours they would be picked up by the German police and turned over to West German Intelligence, where they were threatened with being sent back East, the result being that they rushed back to Camp King apologizing profusely.

Jacks had read her husband's interrogation file and had to corroborate the personal information, then ask her about the Foreign Affairs Ministry, where she had worked in the travel department. Finally, what they asked all defectors: conditions in the German Democratic Republic.

She had it all down pat: told Jacks about her husband's military career – going nowhere because of his lack of motivation, which created suspicion – the names of Foreign Affairs Ministry officials and their travel history, as well as she could remember. Mostly they traveled around the Eastern bloc, including Moscow; only the higher ups went to the west, and they were too important for her to handle. Conditions? She was supposed to tell the truth, and she did: shortages of almost everything, although she was privileged in that respect because of her job in the Ministry. But all her relatives and friends expected her to buy things for them, and she had to ask an official, which she didn't like to do, especially as most of them expected sexual favors in return, which she refused to give. The Stasi informers were everywhere, so there was no freedom of speech, no freedom at all in fact. They had wanted her to be an informer and she refused, which made any possibility for advancement impossible. And everyone knows that the Russians are really in charge, that the so-called German Democratic Republic is nothing but a puppet and the Russians are hated. She added, almost as an afterthought, that if the wall came down the whole population might go over to the west. Did they already know that? She asked herself. Was she going too far?

"Frau Cornelius," her American interrogator was saying. "Is something wrong?" And she realized that there were tears in her eyes and she had almost forgotten his presence.

"No, I'm sorry, it's just that ..."

Marvin Jacks had the impression that she looked familiar, even thought of that young Russian woman he'd met in the bar in San Francisco, and then lost. He'd only been with her for less than a hour and his memory of her was dim, especially because he had been at least half-drunk. It didn't occur to him that this could be the same person.

10 Hamburger Allee

Frankfurt

Lt. Marvin Jacks rented a room in a pension on Hamburger Allee in Frankfurt. He smiled at the street's name. Did it make the love affair sound trite, even ridiculous? In German the reference was to the city of Hamburg, and he had every intention of keeping it a secret as far as his American compatriots were concerned. He didn't want them installing bugs in the room. The only other person who knew about it was the lady in question: Frau Anneliese Cornelius. Lt. Cornelius and frau had been thoroughly debriefed and they were let loose to pursue their lives in West Germany. There was, however, a shade of suspicion, on the part of Master Sergeant Jack Quinn, that they might be Stasi agents.

Quinn hadn't participated in any of the interrogations, but he'd read the reports, as Colonel Banks routinely asked him to do. Then the meeting with Banks and the two interrogators, the other being a First Lt. Hamburg (sic). Although outranked by everyone, Quinn ran the meeting. Hamburg and Jacks had copies of the interrogation reports on their laps; Quinn had no papers. Banks looked bored.

"You guys say you're satisfied these people are on the level, right?" Quinn asked, looking at the two officers one after the other. Actually neither had written exactly that in their reports. Like good bureaucrats covering themselves just in case they had written that they found no indication that the Cornelius couple weren't what they said they were: real defectors. Lt. Hamburg, was annoyed by being treated as a subordinate by an enlisted man, Col. Banks' favorite because he had a good jump shot. He also knew from experience, however, that Quinn had a nose for smelling lies. Not lies exactly – any interrogator worth his salt could do that – but half-truths, which were much harder to detect. Sgt. Quinn could detect them; he called it intuition. And that's why Col. Banks had him read all the interrogation reports before making final decisions. "I found no indication that he isn't," Hamburg said.

"Same difference." Quinn brushed off Hamburg's correction. He questioned Jacks with his eyebrows. "I found nothing in Frau Cornelius's story to think otherwise," Jacks said.

"Well, you might both be right, but something about this bothers me." He looked at Col. Banks, seated behind his large desk, to see if he was paying attention. Banks was. "Go on, Sergeant," he said, stroking his mustache wisely.

"Just for a moment let's assume that they are Stasi agents," Quinn said. "One's an army officer, the other works in the Foreign Ministry, according to their cover story at least. This makes them interesting, right?"

"Certainly does," Col. Banks agreed.

"They cross over and come to us. Why?" He directed the question at Lt. Hamburg.

"Because he's army and we're army," Hamburg replied.

"Right. But why didn't they go to the West German army? Did either of you ask that question?" He shook his head. "Never mind, it's not in your reports. The question, then, is: Why not?"

"Goddammit, Colonel, I wish you'd remind Sgt. Quinn that we're officers and he should address us as such."

Col. Banks raised his eyebrows and smiled ever so faintly. Then, to Quinn: "He's right, Sergeant. But this is an informal meeting, so let's just get on with it."

"Why not ... Lieutenant?" He looked at Jacks.

Jacks suppressed the impulse to address Quinn as Sir, and said that he hadn't thought of it.

"And you?" looking at Hamburg and infuriating him by omission.

"Because the answer is that the West Germans would have kept them in much less comfortable circumstances than we do, and for longer, and would have made him join the West German army to prove his loyalty, and as an Enlisted Man to boot."

"Good reasons to come to us instead," Quinn said, "especially the E.M. part. But how would he know that?"

"The grapevine, Quinn, probably everyone in the East German army knows it – the officers anyway."

"So, you assumed that was the reason and didn't bother to ask, right?"

"Right."

"And you, Lt. Jacks, didn't think of it."

Jacks nodded. He liked and admired Quinn, despite being on the hot-seat, couldn't help it. Anyway, it was his first interrogation, and of the woman, not the army officer, so his seat wasn't that hot.

"But there could be another reason for coming to us instead of the Germans," Quinn went on, "an even better one." He sat back like an actor waiting for his cue. Col. Banks supplied it: "What's that, Sergeant?"

"The Germans are a hell of a lot better at this than we are. Sorry to admit it, Sir, but it's true, inevitable."

"Why inevitable," Col. Banks asked, frowning.

"Because they're Germans, know the German soul, can detect nuances that we can't, know more about the East German army and Stasi. So German Military Intelligence, if there was even the whiff of suspicion, would have turned them over to the *Bundessicherheitsdienst* – their CIA. We don't do that, to us they're guests from hell who have recognized the evils of communism and are now friends. All we want is military information."

"That's not true, Quinn," Hamburg protested. "We look for agents, too, all the time."

"True," Quinn rejoined calmly, "but it's not our priority; it is theirs. Furthermore, we got turnstile interrogators and analysts. You do your tour of duty and leave or are transferred. The draftees go home just when they're beginning to know what they're doing. The Germans aren't going anywhere."

"What's your point, Quinn?" Lt. Hamburg asked after an embarrassing silence.

"I thought it was obvious, Hamburg, but ..."

"Col. Banks!" Hamburg almost shouted.

"We know you're an officer, Hamburg," Banks said calmly. "We can see the bars on your shoulders. Now just shut up and listen."

Hamburg turned beet-red, and probably didn't listen.

"Anyway," Quinn went on, "they may have come to us for the reasons stated by Lt. Hamburg – or they may have come because they wanted to avoid a real, hard-ass interrogation by people who would at least suspect them."

"You mean who have other priorities," Col. Banks said.

"Yes, Sir," Quinn smiled.

"So, what do you suggest?"

"That we keep them under surveillance for a while."

"Ah," the colonel said, "and how do we do that?"

Hamburg woke up. "I can assemble a surveillance team, Sir."

Banks raised his eyebrows and looked at Quinn.

"A two-day course in Munich, which is the amount of training you guys get, doesn't make a surveillance team, Hamburg." Hamburg opened his mouth but nothing came out. "And if they are agents, they've been trained to spot amateur surveillance," Quinn said. "No, we have to do it a different way."

"Er ..."

"Yes, Lt. Jacks?" Col. Banks said.

"Why don't we just turn the case over to the CIA?" It was a rhetorical question; he knew they wouldn't buy it.

Banks smiled and again looked at Quinn. He obviously didn't want to be quoted.

"Because they're worse than us, you can spot them as Americans a mile away. Anyway, they probably wouldn't take it seriously. After all, we have no facts."

"Only your intuition, Sgt. Quinn," Banks said, "and that's good enough for me. What other way?"

"Jacks can come on to the woman. Reading between the lines of his report, I detect a rapport."

Marvin Jacks hoped his face wasn't as red as Hamburg's. They were all looking at him. He'd intended to get in touch with her anyway, now they were asking him to, but for a very different reason.

"Is that the case, Lt. Jacks?" Col. Banks asked.

"Sgt. Quinn is very perceptive," Jacks said with a silly grin, "but yes, we got on well."

"Okay, go on, Sergeant Quinn."

"We check her out for a few days, just to see if there's a pattern of some place she goes where Jacks could bump into her, by accident that is. Then Jacks makes a date with her, starts an affair if possible, finds out if there's anything to my intuition about them."

"What about the husband?" Hamburg said, just to say something.

"Well," Quinn answered, "if she's a loyal wife and or a good agent, Jacks'll get shot down – I don't mean that literally. What do you think about that though, Lt. Jacks?"

"Her husband's not the romantic type," Jacks said. That did get a laugh.

"You willing, Lt. Jacks?" Col. Banks asked.

After a short pretense of thinking it over, "Yes, Sir."

11 Goethe's Complete Works

Quinn had a German driver, a friend of his employed by Camp King, observe Frau Cornelius. He'd been in the Wehrmacht M.I. and had surveillance experience, was also smart. After the first week he reported back that she went to the flea market in Bockenheim two or three times, bought some cheap stuff. Quinn asked him if she might be making a contact there. The driver shrugged. "*Könnte sein*," he said, but he hadn't noticed anything, though he admitted that it would be a perfect place for it. Quinn told Jacks to let her see and approach him, if possible. If she didn't, he should approach her, but if he thought she wanted to avoid him they'd drop the whole thing. "And Jacks," Quinn, damn him, said, but Jacks was used by then to being treated as his subordinate, "remember this is work, so don't fall for her or you might be in trouble, if what I'm thinking is true, that is."

"Don't worry about that, Sgt. Quinn." Why worry, when it had already happened?

The meeting came off perfectly. Jacks went to the Bockenheimer flea market the following Saturday in civvies. It was big and he didn't look out of place, for there were other Americans there, servicemen looking for bargains. He saw her at a used books stand concentrated on a book she was leafing through. He strolled to the other side of the same stand until he was directly across from her. The book she held was the first volume of Goethe's Complete Works. He leaned across and picked up the second volume and opened it. She saw his hand do it of course and looked up.

"Lt. Jacks!" she said.

He looked up innocently and pretended to be trying to place her. Then, "Frau Cornelius, what a surprise!" He walked around the stand and they shook hands.

"Are you interested in Goethe?" she asked him.

"I'd like to be more interested, but he's a bit difficult for me, I need a dictionary at my elbow."

She laughed. "It's a good way to improve your German."

"Undoubtedly. Are you going to buy that book?"

"No, the dealer will only sell the complete set. He's right of course. Why break it up?"

Jacks saw his opening. "Oh? How much does he want?" The dealer, a skinny little man with a huge mustache, was watching them from his seat at the opposite corner of the stand. He smelled a sale.

"A hundred marks. That's frightfully expensive for used books."

"It depends on how you look at it. If they were new they'd cost a lot more, and the words are the same."

"I suppose you're right," she said. "And they are quite beautiful, pre-war, of course."

"Wait here," Jacks told her. He went over to the dealer, greeted him cordially as one must, and asked if he could reserve the complete set with twenty marks, that he would return the next day with the rest of the money.

"*Jawohl, Mein Herr*, you certainly may," the dealer said and held out his hand. Jacks gave him the twenty and he took a piece of cardboard from his pocket, printed GEKAUFT on it, and placed it on the center volume of the set. Jacks wondered if he could get the money back as confidential funds, but immediately decided against asking. She isn't a spy, for God's sake.

"I'll pay him the rest tomorrow and the first volume is yours," he told her when he was again at her side.

"But Lt. Jacks, I couldn't accept that. Besides, you'll want to keep the set complete."

"Maybe you can help me with Goethe's German in return." She smiled, but didn't answer.

"How about a coffee?"

She looked at her watch and said, "I have to go now, but ... When will you pick up the books?"

"It's Sunday tomorrow, so any time really."

"Twelve?"

"Fine, it's a date."

"Auf Wiedersehen, Lt. Jacks," she said and gave him her hand.

"Auf Wiedersehen, Frau Cornelius." He watched her walk away. Not the Germanic type at all, he thought. Dark hair, petite, beautiful in her way.

They met the next day at the book stall, he paid the remainder of the money to the dealer, who wrapped the ten volumes in two packages. She took one, he the other, and they walked off together. It was cold and they were thankful for the warm gemütlich café. Jacks ordered brandy with their coffee. She poured hers into the coffee and insisted that he try it. He did. They stayed there over an hour. One thing led to another. He asked her about her plans now in the west. She said that her husband was thinking of joining the army if they would recognize his commission. She had applied at several places as a secretary, but she had the impression that there was a certain prejudice against people from the east, so it wasn't easy. She also admitted that she was thinking of leaving her husband. He was so, well, military. It wasn't his fault really, but now that she was free, she wanted to be completely so. After a half dozen brandies they went to a nearby hotel and spent another hour there under the eiderdown. Jacks had fallen – hard. He rented the room on Hamburger Allee and they met there almost every day for a month. Then she disappeared.

That last day in their room on Hamburger Allee, Anneliese was especially loving, sexually and, later, tenderly. Jacks felt tears on her cheeks, but ascribed it to his love making technique which, if the truth be told, was amateurish compared to hers. He wondered if experience or natural talent had been her teacher – but he didn't ask. The next day she didn't show, nor the next. He noticed that both Goethe volumes, which they had begun reading together, were gone. Her phone didn't answer and when he went to her apartment the landlord told him that Herr and Frau Cornelius had moved out two days ago, without leaving a forwarding address.

12 Third Encounter

Buenos Aires, Argentina

Marvin Jacks had bought a house in the town of Florida – emphasis on the "i" in Spanish – a suburb of Buenos Aires. He was now the International Air Transport Association's Director of Security and Fraud Detection for the whole Western Hemisphere, but there was an Assistant Director in Miami who handled most of the North American cases, and reported to Jacks in Buenos Aires instead of directly to Head Office in Geneva. Jacks had fought tooth and nail to avoid being moved to head office, claiming he could do the job better in the field, which was certainly true. Finally it came down to a duel between him and the Finance Director, whose idea of efficiency was to move everyone to head office and let them perform their miracles with modern communications technology. Jacks finally won by getting the support of the president of the national carrier, Argentine Airlines, a general who owed him a favor. That particular officer is still in jail for human rights abuses, so it wouldn't be politic to mention his name or the favor here. The Director General of IATA personally overruled the Finance Director, whom he hated, after receiving a telephone call from the general, during which he, the general, said Marvin Jacks' continued presence in Buenos Aires was essential to the survival of the airline industry – or words to that effect. Argentine generals are known to exaggerate.

Florida was originally settled by German immigrants at the beginning of the twentieth century. The Second World War saw an influx of Germans, war veterans who had no wish to live in a destroyed Germany, Nazis, a few Socialists who had somehow survived the Third Reich, and some Jews who couldn't get into Israel because of the British blockade. There had been Jews among the original settlers, so it wasn't unnatural that these post-concentration camp German Jews also inclined towards Florida, although the majority settled in Buenos Aires itself.

All that didn't interest Marvin Jacks. He liked the place because it was clean and, at the time, property was relatively cheap there. Most of his time was spent traveling, but when he was in Buenos Aries at least he had a quiet place to sleep and restful weekends with a swimming pool and plenty of sun. Women occasionally served to assuage his solitude. They were mostly airline employees, at that time still called stewardesses rather than the politically correct "flight attendants," or the more grounded airport personnel. None became permanent, perhaps because Marvin Jacks wasn't permanent himself.

For public relations purposes airlines often gave cocktail parties, each company at least once a year, which meant an average of two a month. As the IATA representative, Jacks was always invited. Sometimes he went, sometimes he didn't. He was also invited to lunch, something he couldn't refuse, although such invitations were seldom repeated because he never invited back. IATA had no budget for such things and he wasn't selling anything anyway. The airline managers invited him in order to stay on his good side and, if possible, to obtain information. They received none, but Jacks did, and that was his main reason for accepting. The food didn't interest him, it never did, but the wine, dessert and a good after-lunch Cuban cigar made everything bearable.

And that brings us to Freddy Hussein. Freddy was the Lebanese General Sales Agent for LAN Chile. An unusual position, because LAN had its own ticket office and Chilean manager. Why, then, did they need a General Sales Agent as well? GSAs normally existed when the airline didn't have its own sales office. The reason, it was generally assumed, was that LAN wanted Freddy because he was a good salesman, but couldn't very well have a non-Chilean as manager. Marvin Jacks didn't buy that, but didn't care because LAN was not an important player in the market. He wondered though, how a Lebanese who didn't even speak Spanish could be a good salesman in a Spanish-speaking country, and decided it had something to do with politics. It didn't occur to him at first that Freddy Hussein could be a spy.

Freddy often phoned Jacks asking for interpretations of IATA rules, thereby admitting that he didn't know much about the business. He also invited him to lunch every time he called. Jacks begged off with invented excuses, something he couldn't do when an important airline manager was doing the inviting. Finally, at an Air France cocktail party, Freddy insisted so much that Jacks agreed.

"There's an excellent German restaurant in Florida," he said. "Do you like German food?"

Marvin Jacks didn't particularly like German food, pastries yes, but the fact that Freddy Hussein was inviting him to lunch in Florida caused him to put down his martini unfinished in order to be alert. Did Freddy know he lived in Florida? He hadn't told any business associates, never gave out his home telephone number. Before he could think of a reply though, Freddy was telling him that he would pick him up at his office at twelve-thirty the next day. "It's only fifteen minutes to Florida by car," he said, as if Jacks didn't know. So maybe he wasn't aware that Jacks lived there.

Next day the phone rang at 12:25. Freddy Hussein's secretary: "Mr. Hussein is leaving now Mr. Jacks. He asks if you can wait downstairs, so he won't lose time parking."

A chauffeur-driven Mercedes Benz. Freddy Hussein did okay for the GSA of a third world airline. That was just one of the thoughts that ran through Marvin Jacks' head as Freddy talked incessantly on the way to the restaurant "Die Glocke" in Florida. The chauffeur dropped them off at the entrance on Florida's main drag and disappeared. The restaurant was small but well appointed. About ten tables, each with fresh, real flowers in vases on them. An aging, white clad, bow-tied waiter with a German accent greeted them at the door, Jacks in Spanish, then, to Hussein in German: "So nice to see you again, Herr Hussein. I will tell Frau Marie that you are here." He seated them at a corner table. Jacks' instinct told him to keep his back to the wall, but the waiter was holding the back-to-the-door chair for Freddy Hussein who, it seemed, had similar instincts. The waiter recommended *Eisbein*, the specialty of the day, which Hussein accepted but Jacks passed on and selected *Grüne Sosse*, a Frankfurt specialty consisting of potatoes covered in herb sauce.

"Do you prefer German or Argentine wine, Mr. Jacks?" Hussein asked.

"Argentine, no contest."

Hussein laughed. "A wise choice."

"You speak German, Mr. Hussein?"

"Not really. Heinz greets all the guests in German, for atmosphere you know, like the waiters in Italian restaurants always say Bon giorno. Your Spanish seems excellent, I wish I could get the hang of it."

"Well, I've been here a long time."

"So, I've heard," Hussein said. "Isn't that unusual? Foreign managers are usually transferred on after a few years."

"Just fate I guess."

Hussein laughed his high-pitched, hyena laugh. "Fate, yes, a wonderful concept. Do you think it exists?"

"I don't know, but at least it provides answers to the imponderables of life."

"That's interesting. I've often wondered if what I do is really determined by me or … well … fate. Did you ever ask yourself that question, Mr. Jacks?"

Marvin Jacks had asked himself just that many times, but he wasn't about to get personal with Freddy Hussein. "No," he said. Hussein looked up from Jack's gaze and smiled: "Ah, Frau Marie." He jumped up and held out the chair between him and Jacks, who stood up for the coming introduction.

"Frau Marie, may I present my colleague, Mr. Marvin Jacks, a very important person in the airline business." She turned her smile to Jacks and it froze. Her hand was out to be shook but Jacks didn't take it until Freddy Hussein, as an afterthought, said, "Mr. Jacks, this is Frau Marie, the owner of this wonderful eatery and wife of the best chef in Buenos Aires, which means of course in Argentina." Jacks took her hand, but couldn't say a word, his head was whirling. Nor did she. "Please sit with us a moment, Frau Marie," Hussein said. If he wondered why they were staring at each other without a word, he may have attributed it to hormonal fascination, for Frau Marie was indeed beautiful.

Hussein snapped his fingers for Heinz, the waiter, and asked him to bring another wine glass, then, when it arrived, proposed a toast: "To a meeting of cultures." Marvin Jacks and Frau Marie, once known as Judith Baumgartner and somewhat later as Anneliese Cornelius, drank considerably more than the traditional sip. Freddy Hussein was finding it hard keeping up three sides of the conversation, so decided to force participation. "Mr. Jacks is American but has been in Argentina a long time, isn't it so, Mr. Jacks?"

"Yes, but not *so* long," Jacks mumbled.

"Oh? How long?" Frau Marie asked.

"Seven years."

"You must like it here then."

"One gets used to it. How about you?"

She smiled for the first time. "On and off. We came here fifteen years ago, but those were difficult times, you know, so we went back to Germany after a while. We earned some money there and came back with the idea of opening a restaurant. And well, we did." It was like a script she had often repeated.

"We?" Jacks said.

"My husband Karl-Heinz and I. He learned to cook in Germany."

As though on cue, Karl-Heinz appeared at their table and greeted them with a slight bow in broken Spanish, and rushed back to the kitchen. Jacks had seen Lt. Cornelius through the one-way interrogation-room window at Camp King, but Cornelius, if he had ever seen Jacks at all, it was only as another soldier walking around the camp. Jacks thought he must have heard his name though.

Before the food arrived Freddy Hussein's chauffeur came rushing in and said something to him in Arabic. "Oh, dear, isn't this awful," Hussein said, standing up. "A crisis has arisen and I must go immediately. Most unfortunate, my deepest apologies, Mr. Jacks. Frau Marie, could you be so kind as to entertain my guest?" He scurried out. Jacks finished off his second glass of wine and said, in German, "Okay, so what the hell is going on, Anneliese?"

She said, in English, smiling: "Do you mind if I sit with you a while, Mr. Jacks? It gives me an excuse to rest before the lunch crowd arrives."

Jacks blinked. Games. "Sure, be my guest, Frau Marie." The waiter appeared at his side and refilled the wine glasses. They raised their glasses, staring into each other's eyes, German style.

"Argentine wine is really very good, the reds at least. It's a pity they aren't better known outside the country."

"Organization," Jacks said. "You may have noticed that this country isn't very well organized."

She smiled and was about to agree, but Jacks said, "not like Germany."

"Yes, that's true. Germany is a bit too organized for my taste."

"Is that why you're here?"

"Partly, yes."

"What's the other part?"

"My husband inherited a piece of land here and we came to see about it and, well, we fell in love with the country."

"Convenient."

Her eyes frowned warning, but just for a moment, until she smiled again and said, "Yes, fate can sometimes be convenient."

"But not always."

She laughed falsely, as though he had told the funniest joke of the day. "Do you like philosophy, Mr. Jacks?"

"Not any more. I used to be an idealist, now I'm a naïve realist. How about you?"

"Oh, it's all too deep for me. I prefer novels."

"Good, so do I. Too bad Goethe wrote so few of them"

Two middle-aged, straight-backed men entered and bowed towards them. "Guten Tag," Frau Marie called to them and waved. Gradually the restaurant was filling up. Jacks was served his grüne Sosse and another glass of wine.

"Actually, the Germans were very big in philosophy," Jacks said, "until Marx at least."

"Marx just about finished off German philosophy, except possibly for Rudolf Steiner, ever heard of him?"

"The name sounds familiar."

"There's a Rudolf Steiner School right here in Florida. Did you know that? My daughter goes there."

"Oh yes, I know, about the school, that is."

"Do you have any children, Mr. Jacks?"

"No."

"You're not married?"

"No."

"How do you know about the school then?"

"A friend's kid goes there."

"Oh? What's his name? Maybe I know your friend."

"I don't think so. Please don't let me keep you from your duties, Frau Marie," with ironic emphasis on her current name.

"Yes, I really must go now. We have excellent *Schwarzwaldtorte* for dessert."

"Homemade?"

"Yes ... but not by me."

"In that case I'll pass. Could you just send the bill, please?"

"Mr. Hussein has taken care of it." She stood up. "We could advise you when we have specials, Mr. Jacks, and German delicacies, made by me, if you'll give me your phone number."

Jacks looked up at her and couldn't help thinking of Ingrid Bergman. He hesitated, stood to be polite, then reached into his wallet and handed her a business card. "I'll be leaving then."

"You haven't finished your lunch."

"Potatoes are filling." She offered her hand. "Should I kiss it?" he asked.

"That would be out of character, wouldn't it?"

"Good bye, then." He turned and walked out before the old waiter could hobble to the door to open it for him. Outside in the heat he felt like fainting, but he walked like a man in a hurry down the street intending to go home, shower and think. Hussein's chauffeur was calling him from behind though. He stopped. "Mr. Hussein told me to wait for you, Señor."

"Give him my thanks, but I prefer to walk awhile."

"I can wait."

"No. Adios."

He walked past the street his house was on, circled around the block, making sure he wasn't being followed, turned back and went home. Once inside, he walked through the living room, ignoring the blinking answering machine, shedding a piece of clothing in each room until he was in the garden in the rear. He gazed into the water in the pool – clear, limpid, uncomplicated, just how he wished his mind could be. As he was about to dive in, a breeze arose rippling the water and brushing aside the clarity. He dove naked into the irony. It refreshed him, but didn't clear his confusion. He called his office and told his secretary that he wasn't feeling well and wouldn't be there that afternoon, she should let him know if anything urgent happened.

"Sorry, Marvin. Do you need anything?"

"No, Amalia, I'll be all right in the morning." Amalia would have loved to take a taxi to Florida and tend to her boss at home. Some other time, Jacks thought. He went to bed and, to his surprise, slept like a log.

At around four the phone rang. "Marvin, a woman called for you and when I told her you weren't in, she asked where she could contact you, that it was urgent," Amalia said. "She was really insistent, as though it was a matter of life and death – so finally I said I'd ask you if I could give her your number. Was that all right? She's going to call back soon."

"What's her name?" Jacks said after his daytime memory returned and wiped out an exciting dream forever.

"María Alemán is what she said."

"Did she have an accent?"

"A little bit, I think."

"Give her my number when she calls," Jacks said. "Thanks, Amalia."

"Okay. You all right, Marvin?"

"Yes, fine." He hung up.

It wasn't until five-thirty that Amalia called again. "She didn't call back, Marvin. I have to go now."

"Any other calls?" Jacks asked, just to cover his disappointment.

"Nothing that can't wait."

"Okay, Amalia. See you tomorrow morning."

13 The CIA Comes Aboard

It may seem far-fetched to relate that these two people, Marvin Jacks and Judith Baumgarten, a.k.a. Anneliese Cornelius and now, apparently, Marie Alemán or, as we shall soon see, Clement, should meet again in another, quite opposite part of the world. Much too fortuitous and convenient for this story to be believed. Nevertheless, such things happen more frequently than you'd expect. Marvin and the then Anneliese were truly in love back in Germany when they were both very young. When Anneliese seemingly disappeared from the face of the earth Marvin Jacks was devastated. Anneliese perhaps (how can we know?) even more so. The fact that they were living double lives spying on each other made them both suspect that they had been found out, which bothered their mutual consciences, although they were mistaken. Jacks had been ordered to keep an eye on Anneliese just in case she was more than an innocent East German refugee, and Anneliese, once her masters realized that Jacks was attracted to her, had ordered her to keep him on a string, find out what she could from him, even try to recruit him if it seemed possible. Now they were afraid that it might be starting all over again.

Anneliese, now Frau Marie, saw it coming as soon as she saw him, for she had been expecting Freddy Hussein to bring an American airline official to lunch in order to seduce him. Motive? They suspected he was

CIA, at least Freddy Hussein had a hunch that he was. He couldn't believe that an American who spoke three languages (he'd found out from the Lufthansa manager that Jacks spoke German), living in Argentina and flying around Latin America and other parts of the world in a job that seemed, to him, without tangible objectives, could be only what he claimed to be. The job could therefore be a cover. If he was right it would be a feather in his cap; if he was wrong ... well ... what did he have to lose? Certainly not Frau Marie's virginity.

Marvin Jacks didn't see it coming until he received a phone call the next morning from John Armstrong, the Panam manager, who asked him to stop by his office at his convenience, which usually meant asap. Such calls were routine and were almost always motivated by an airline manager wanting to complain to Jacks about a competitor giving discounts or ask for his interpretation of an IATA rule, although the interpretation could usually be handled by phone, so Jacks expected the former reason. He was reluctant to leave the office and possibly miss another call from Frau Marie, but couldn't stall Armstrong, at least not in good conscience, so he told him he'd be right over. Panam was, after all, one of the most important airlines in the market. He told his secretary he'd be back in an hour.

Armstrong ushered him into his office, had him sit in one of the leather easy chairs in the corner near the large window overlooking the Rio de la Plata, and offered him Colombian coffee and a Cuban cigar. Jacks accepted the coffee, passed on the cigar. He knew the corner was reserved for government ministers, important travel agents and clients. So, Armstrong wanted something, otherwise Jacks would be sitting across from him at his desk. He was a tall, thin man with a receding widow's peak and hooked nose. His clothes had obviously been bought in the U.S. – loafers, pants not quite touching his shoe tops, button-down collar on a white shirt, regimental-stripe silk tie.

"Marvin, we've known each other a long time now," he began. "How long has it been? Years. And we've grown to respect each other as honorable men, Americans to the core." Jacks was immediately wary. He remembered how a few years earlier a Latvian friend who also lived in Argentina had confided to him that he once did some work for the CIA, and that Armstrong was his handler. The friend was rabidly anti-Soviet, as were all émigrés from the Baltic countries, so the CIA had no hesitation in recruiting them. They paid him a hundred dollars a month to "keep his ears open." He accepted the money for six months but never heard anything to report, so his employment was terminated. Jacks had forgotten about it and was never sure if it was true anyway.

"So, I'm going to tell you something now in strict confidentiality," Armstrong continued. "Can I depend on your keeping this to yourself?" IATA's policy was never to divulge the name of the complaining airline when information was given about a competitor's misdeeds. Armstrong knew this, so Jacks decided it was something else. But he said anyway, "You know our policy, John. That's not a problem."

"This has nothing to do with business, Marvin." He opened an ivory inlaid cigarette box and offered it to Jacks, knowing he didn't smoke cigarettes. Jacks shook his head and took his pipe from a side pocket of his suit jacket. The pocket was strewn with loose tobacco and ashes, which he made a mental note to empty once outside. He took a tobacco pouch from another pocket, filled the pipe and lit it with a Zippo. They blew smoke at each other and waited to see who would blink. It was Armstrong.

"Can I, Marvin?"

"I have to know what it is first, John. I'm sure you can understand that."

"Yes, I can." He sighed histrionically. "Okay, I know I can trust you Marvin, so here goes." He took a deep drag on his cigar, let the smoke out from his nose and said, "I lead a double life, Marvin. You see, I also work for our government." He waited. Jacks had to say something.

"I see. In what capacity?"

"Central Intelligence Agency."

If he'd expected Jacks to fall over in astonishment, he was mistaken. Instead, Jacks said, "Good for you, but what's that got to do with me?"

"A lot, Marvin. We want you to help us."

"Are you trying to recruit me, John?"

Armstrong laughed as though he were enjoying the repartee, which he wasn't. "Not exactly ... or in a sense yes, but just for one case ... although if you were interested after that, well, who knows?" Jacks started to say something, but Armstrong wasn't finished. "You will be paid for your time of course ... and, Marvin, that's the first thing I would like you to keep secret – my association with the Agency."

"Sure, no problem."

"Good. Thanks. I know you were in military intelligence in the army and had a distinguished record."

"That's news to me," Jacks said.

"That you were in M.I.?" Armstrong said, frowning, suddenly awake to the possibility that they'd checked the wrong man.

"No, that I had a distinguished record. Didn't do anything distinguished that I can remember."

"Well, let's just say that your record is clean, that you were in interrogation, then special ops, meaning sending spies – I think you call them 'sources' in the army – into East Germany, and debriefing them afterward. Right?"

"Something like that," Jacks replied, thinking back to those times and, inevitably, Anneliese.

"I love that answer, Marvin. It shows reserve and a sense of confidentiality even now."

This guy is too much, Jacks thought. Why don't I politely tell him to fuck off and get the hell out of here. "Not much to be confidential about," he said though, wanting to keep his options open while he pondered the alternatives. "We couldn't find a gas mask in a gas mask store."

"A gas mask?"

"Somehow the C.O. got information – probably from the Pentagon – that the Russians had a new gas mask that had been distributed to their troops in East Germany. So, we were given the job of getting one. Why? Because it was there, I guess, like a mountain." His pipe had gone out as it often did when he was talking, so he re-lighted it.

"So, what happened?" Armstrong asked. "Did you get it?"

Jacks laughed. "No, we tried for over a year, until I left at least. Maybe they're still trying." He was curious about what they wanted him to do and that was so important that they checked his army record before even asking if he was open to the possibility. He decided to play it cool.

"I don't know, John. I've had enough of that stuff, I think."

Armstrong saw the opening in the last two words. "And I think you think wrong. It gets into your blood, man. We all know that."

Curiosity turned to apprehension and his heart jumped. Could this have something to do with Anneliese? Armstrong was wrong about his blood though. He had really had enough of the cloak and dagger circus and, most of all, the people involved who seemed to like it. But ...

"What do you want me to do?"

Armstrong slapped him on the knee. "Atta boy, I knew you were a patriot."

"Wait a minute, John," Jacks said. "I only asked you what you want. I didn't say I'd do it. First of all, why did you think of me?"

"Right, Marvin, I'll open up – totally. You were seen going into a restaurant in Florida" – he opened a pocket notebook: "Die Glocke – the other day with Freddy Hussein. Tuesday as a matter of fact, at twelve-thirty hours. Hussein left at twelve-forty five, alone, and you left at thirteen-fifteen, also alone. You went into a house there in Florida via a circuitous route, walking. You had the key. Is that right?"

"Sounds right, so what?"

"Could you tell me why?"

"Why what?"

"Why you went to that particular restaurant with Hussein."

"What the hell is this, an interrogation? Should I call my lawyer? Why were you following me?"

Armstrong smiled, having expected this kind of reaction. "No, Marvin," he said, "it isn't an interrogation. But you asked me why we thought of you. And we weren't following you. We were following Freddy Hussein."

Jacks thought a moment, but he had already decided that he'd have to find out what was going on. "Okay, I was there with Hussein because he invited me for lunch. In fact he'd invited me several times, and I always gave some excuse. He's a pest, you know. So finally this time I thought I'd get it over with. He picked me up at my office in his car and we drove to Florida. He said he knew a great German restaurant there. I didn't have much choice."

"What about the house?"

"In Florida? I live there."

"You live in Florida?"

"Yeah, anything wrong with that?"

"No, of course not. But you have no family – as far as I know – so I expected you'd live in an apartment in the Calle Florida in town rather than in a suburb."

"I like it there."

"Sure," Armstrong said, smiling falsely again. "No offense meant. Why did Hussein leave before you, and quite early?"

"His chauffeur came in and told him something in Arabic, some kind of emergency I guess, so Freddy said he had to leave, apologies, etcetera." Jacks wondered if the conversation was being recorded. He guessed it was. So far, he'd told Armstrong nothing but the truth.

"Uh huh." Armstrong looked down at his notebook. "Did anything happen in the restaurant?"

"Like what?"

"Like anything. Did you talk to anyone?"

"Only the owner, a Frau Marie."

"Marie Clement, wife of Karl-Heinz Clement. He's the cook. What did you and Frau Marie talk about?"

"Small talk, nothing." There goes the truth, he thought.

"Small talk isn't nothing, Marvin. Think."

"She was sort of filling in for Hussein after he left. I don't know, she asked me what airline I was with, and I explained IATA to her. She told me this was the second time they'd been to Argentina, that she loved it but everything was complicated. The usual. Oh, that she's from Hamburg I think she said."

"Anything else?"

"No, some people came in and she went to butter them up, seems like a good hostess. Now what's this about, John?"

"Just one more question first. Why did you take the long way home?"

"I wanted to walk off the meal. I was very tired and decided to take the afternoon off. Don't tell my boss."

Armstrong laughed as though it were the best joke of the season. "Don't worry, I wouldn't think of it," he said. "Now, what this is all about." He paused for effect and looked Jacks in the eye for too long. "Freddy Hussein is a spy."

"Doesn't surprise me," Jacks said. "For whom?"

"We're not sure, probably one of the East European intelligence services."

"Too dumb for the Soviets?"

"Maybe."

"How do you know?"

"We know."

"Okay."

"He goes frequently to Die Glocke, seems to know the Clements well, which makes us suspicious of them as well."

"Any other reason to suspect them?" Jacks asked.

"Not really. Oh yes, according to one of our German sources she talks more like an easterner than a Hamburger" – he smiled gloomily at the little joke – "from Berlin perhaps."

"Maybe she was originally from Berlin and moved to Hamburg."

"Possibly. That's about all we know, but we'd like to know more. That's why I'm asking you to help us."

"How could I help?" Jacks asked.

"Freddy Hussein takes you to Die Glocke. He didn't know you live in Florida, right?"

"Right."

"I wonder why. Any ideas?"

"He said the food was great."

"Was it?"

"Well, it's probably the only restaurant in Argentina where you can get *grüne Sosse*."

"What's that?"

"A German dish," Jacks replied. "The food's good there, but I'm not a gourmet."

"He doesn't have to go to Florida for good food, does he?"

"Why then?"

"You're American, you have good contacts in the airline business, the police, probably even S.I.D.E., a mysterious job. Why not try to recruit you? Or maybe you're already one of us. Why not try to find out? If so, even better, try and turn you around."

"How?"

"I understand that Frau Marie is a very attractive, interesting woman."

Jacks was surprised; he didn't have to pretend. "Do you have any facts that lead you to such a conclusion, John, or is your imagination getting the better of you?"

"Why else would Hussein bring you out to Florida for lunch, introduce you to Marie Clements and disappear with a silly excuse? You tell me."

Jacks' pipe had gone out, so he lighted it again. Considering what he knew about the lady now known as Marie Clements, Armstrong was probably right.

"By the way, Marvin," Armstrong said, "you might be out of a job soon, so that's more reason to consider ... "

"Why's that?"

"I received a telex from New York just before you walked in. Didn't have much time to think about it, but it doesn't look good. It seems the U.S. CAB has revoked IATA's anti-trust immunity – or is about to; the wording isn't too clear."

Jacks and Armstrong stared at each other. It meant that the airlines could no longer set fares among themselves under the umbrella of IATA's anti-trust immunity. "Damn fools," Jacks finally said.

"The CAB?"

"They're political, fools or not. I mean the airlines. Anyone in the business with any sense could see this coming. But what did we do? Nothing."

"What could we have done?"

"Bring the consumers – passengers and air freight shippers – into the process. I recommended it a year ago."

"But no one listened?"

"They listened but thought the European governments could pressure the United States not to go that route. They didn't realize that the U.S. couldn't care less what anyone else thinks. It's gonna be dog eat dog now, John." He was thinking that he probably had enough on his platter with security and fraud detection to keep working without tariff compliance. Panam, and John Armstrong with it, on the other hand was in deep trouble. Was it possible that they didn't realize it yet?

"Yeah, well, back to Frau Marie," Armstrong said. "We'd like you to contact her again somehow and try to see what she's up to."

"If anything."

"Right, if anything. What do you say, Marvin?"

Marvin Jacks knew his answer would be yes, but he also knew how to play the game. "Let me sleep on it, John," he said.

"One night?"

"Yeah, I'll let you know tomorrow."

14 International Air Transport Association

"Madelaine Albrecht, IATA Geneva," Jacks' secretary, Amalia, called to him with her hand over her receiver. Their offices were so small that they only used the intercom system when someone from outside was present.

"Madelaine Albrecht – who the hell is that?" Jacks mumbled to himself as he picked up his phone. She spoke in English with a Swiss accent, but he recognized her anyway. "Good morning, Marvin. I'm arriving tomorrow morning on Swissair. Please don't pick me up, Argentine Airlines insists on having that honor."

Think fast, Marvin. "Fine, Madelaine, the Swiss get up too early for me anyway. What time and where should we meet?"

"Midday will be fine, I sleep badly on airplanes. You did make the hotel reservation for me, I hope. Sheraton, wasn't it?"

"Of course."

"Call me before you come, in case I'm still asleep – and don't forget to bring the pertinent files with you. We can have lunch in my room."

"Even though it's all in my head?"

"Yes, Marvin, even if it's all in your head."

"Have a good flight, Madelaine. See you tomorrow."

"Noonish."

"Right."

She thinks my phone is tapped, Jacks thought. And if it is, whoever is listening didn't hear any hotel reservation being made. "Amalia," he called, "make a reservation for Mrs. Madelaine Albrecht at the Sheraton, in tomorrow for one night. IATA discount. I forgot all about it.

"Who is she, Marvin?"

"Some new consultant working with the Human Resources Director. The usual bullshit."

"What usual bullshit?"

"Never mind. Just make the reservation – and get the room number."

15 Revelation

Dawn had finally arrived. Streaks of light probed stealthily through the room, hurried under chairs and tables like a spy with little time left. Marvin Jacks had hardly slept, so he was sitting in the dining room drinking his third coffee, thinking hard and getting nowhere or somewhere, he couldn't decide which. One: Anneliese/Marie was playing it very cloak and dagger, pretending on the telephone to be someone from IATA Geneva. It was good, but not very. If someone wanted to check it would be easy to find out that no such person existed. But they'd have to be suspicious first, and why should they be. Two: the CIA, in the person of John Armstrong, was suspicious of her. Three: Marvin Jacks was also suspicious. Conclusion: she's still a spy for the German Democratic Republic. Big question: Was the rendezvous with him today at the Sheraton part of her clandestine duties, or was all the caution because it was above and beyond duty? No answer. Four: Was Marvin Jacks still in love with her? His head told him he better not be; his heart chuckled and told the truth, for better or for worse. He was. Five: Was she still in love with him, or, more accurately, was she ever? No answer. Six: Did John Armstrong know more than he told Jacks? No answer, but probably not. Seven: How should he answer Armstrong's offer to work for the CIA in order to find out about Anneliese? The answer would have to wait until after his meeting with her this afternoon.

Jacks had been writing it all down on a piece of paper like a question-answer quiz. The result was more questions than answers, but at least now he knew what they were. He held a match to the paper and let the ashes fall into an ashtray. His head leaned slowly onto his chest and his eyes closed. At nine o'clock the phone rang. Jacks shook his head to get his bearings and answered on the fifth ring. "Marvin," Amalia said, "are you okay?"

"Basically yes," he answered. "Slight headache, that's all."

"Mr. Armstrong of Panam already called twice. I told him you should be in any minute. He wants you to call him urgently."

"If he calls again tell him that I had to go to … uh … Montevideo and that I'll probably be back late this afternoon."

"Really, Marvin?"

"Sure. Just tell him that, Amalia."

"I could say you're sick."

"Tell him what I just told you, it's true," Jacks insisted, thinking about the possibility that the phones were tapped. He hung up and turned on the answering machine in case Armstrong got hold of his unlisted home number, which wouldn't be difficult. He had breakfast, showered, dressed, put Mozart on and went to his bookcase to select a book and kill time. To his own surprise he chose Plato over John Le Carré.

For I am quite ready to admit, Simmias and Cebes, that I ought to be grieved at death, if I were not persuaded in the first place that I am going to other gods who are wise and good (of which I am as certain as I can be of any such matters), and secondly (though I am not so sure of this last) to men departed, better than those whom I leave behind; and therefore I do not grieve as I might have done, for I have good

*hope that there is yet something remaining for the dead, and as has
been said of old, some far better thing for the good than for the evil.*

"Socrates was an optimist, Plato," Jacks said to himself. Having
lived alone most of his life he had gotten into the habit of addressing
authors out loud. "Or are you the optimist and Socrates just your
fictional mouthpiece?" If so, you did a good job. Know why? Because
we'll never know." He straightened his tie and put on his suit jacket,
then checked his appearance in the bathroom mirror. "How do I look,
mirror, mirror on the wall? Good enough for whatever her name is?"
He thought of shaving off his beard, which was showing signs of gray,
to make himself look younger, then cursed himself for an idiot,
slammed the bathroom door as well as the outside door and climbed
into his red Mitsubishi. If it's possible to tell a person's character by the
car he owns, Marvin Jacks would be pegged as a practical traditionalist,
which wouldn't be far from wrong.

He parked in his usual place, a parking lot around the corner from
the office. "Little late today, Señor Hacks?" the attendant commented.

"Time is relative, Pedro. I could be early." Pedro frowned at that.
Then, as Jacks was walking out, he said, "Mr. Hacks, a question."

"What is it, Pedro?"

"You have a moment?" Jacks looked at his watch. He had more than
a moment. "Sure."

"Well, you know the Banco de la Nación he is paying almost fifty
percent interest on what you call them ... time deposits?"

"Yes, so?"

"I have some money saved, and I was thinking maybe ... maybe I
should put it in the Banco and then I have a lot more. What do you
think?"

"I think it's a big risk, Pedro."

"Risk? Why? It's in dollars."

"They're paying such high interest rates because no one wants to put their money there at normal rates. Fifty percent is for three months, the yearly rate is a hundred and eighty percent." Pedro frowned harder. He didn't understand.

"But that is the Banco de la Nación, Señor Hacks."

"Uh, huh, and who is the president of the Nación? Never mind. Look, you might make some money on it, all I'm saying is that it's a risk. *Entiende?*"

"Sí señor, muchas gracias."

Thousands of people are putting their miserable little hoards in the bank, Jacks thought as he walked down Florida Street towards Retiro, the central train terminal. The big money is already out, moved to Miami or Zurich. If the Argentine treasury doesn't go broke in thirty days and Pedro takes his double or nothing out then, he wins. If not he loses big, not much money, but all he has.

Retiro terminal is located directly across from the ex-*Plaza Británica*, now the *Plaza Fuerza Aérea Argentina*, on the other side of which is the imposing steel and glass slab known as the Buenos Aires Sheraton. Why did she choose the Sheraton of all places? Jacks wondered. Maybe because of its proximity to Retiro. If she took the train to town, she'd have only to cross the plaza and enter the hotel. Less chance of meeting people she knows. Could be that simple. It's also where an IATA person would go. Would she know that? He walked into the terminal, a huge European style structure. It reminded him of the Milan terminal, the same people running about like ants. He shrugged, lit his pipe and went to the terminal's café. He sat by a large window facing the bustling exhaust-filled street with a direct view across the plaza to the Sheraton. It was too far away to identify anyone entering, but he would certainly recognize her leaving the terminal and crossing the plaza.

Jacks' mind had wandered back to Frankfurt and their room on Hamburger Allee, where they made love every day for a month before she disappeared, simply didn't show up, and neither he, the German police, nor M.I. had been able to find her or her husband. He finished his breakfast of croissants – called *medialunas*, half-moons, in Argentina – juice and coffee, and concentrated more on the stream of people coming from the terminal and passing by his window. Because of the dirty-blond wig and sunglasses, he almost missed her. But he recognized her walk, something lopsided about it. He remembered her mentioning that one leg was a little shorter than the other. She didn't cross to the park, but kept on the street parallel to it, waited with the crowd at the red light, crossed and headed up the hill towards Avenida Santa Fe, Buenos Aires's main shopping street. Must be going on a roundabout route through the crowds in order to double back to the hotel, Jacks thought. Jesus is she being careful, wig and all. He looked at the large clock on the opposite wall and checked it with his watch: eleven o'clock. She said noonish, okay he'd give her an hour, then go to the Sheraton to see if she'd checked in yet. A perfectly normal question for him to ask about his colleague. She had no baggage though. How would she explain that? Well, she's not dumb, that's for sure. Of course, she couldn't just walk in, she'd have to come by taxi, so she probably went to pick up a suitcase somewhere, then take a taxi back to the hotel.

Jacks paid for his breakfast and went into the terminal proper and walked through it slowly against the flow of arriving passengers. The flow would begin to move in the opposite direction after seven o'clock in the evening. It occurred to him that it was remarkable how one could walk through a crowd of moving bodies without bumping into any of them. Some kind of inner radar must be functioning. He had the sensation that he was inside his body instead of being a unity of outside-inside. "He," Jacks, was like a pilot in the cockpit of his head and his body was on automatic, threading itself through darting obstacles, avoiding crashes. He, his "I," was merely an observer. He felt he could have risen to the high arched terminal ceiling and continue watching from there if he willed it enough. But he didn't try; he stayed inside his head. Then Anneliese re-entered his thoughts, not Frau Marie, but the younger Anneliese from the Frankfurt time, and his state of self-awareness popped. He looked up at the huge terminal clock which, however, wasn't working, as usual. His watch read twelve o'clock. He had been wandering back and forth in the terminal for almost an hour.

It struck him as he was leaving the terminal that he didn't have his attaché-case. Damn, he was supposed to be bringing some papers. Was it important? Only if his phone was tapped and he was being followed. Cursing himself for paranoid, he decided to go to the office and pick up his attaché-case and play the role to the hilt. It would only take fifteen minutes.

"Mr. Armstrong called again, Marvin," Amalia said when he walked in. "I told him you were in Montevideo."

Jacks opened the file cabinet in Amalia's office and took out the file marked "Admin-expenses," knowing that she would check on which file he took and that one was as good as any. "Be back later."

"Mrs. Albrecht also called – about ten minutes ago." Jacks turned and stared at her. "She said she was in the Sheraton, room ... she looked at a note paper on her desk "... 712, and that she's expecting you."

Jacks left without acknowledging the message. He walked across the Plaza San Martin without looking at the huge iron statue of the Great Liberator pointing west on its pedestal. He walked through the hotel's lobby, which could have been in any country in the world, to the elevators and pressed the button for the seventh floor.

He had it all rehearsed, what he was going to say to her, and how. All right, Anneliese, what's this all about? For starters. He'd just stand there with his hands in his pockets, one hand anyway, the other holding the file. Cold, cool, the offended party. But it didn't work out that way. She opened the door to room 712 and stepped back. The blond wig was off, and her black hair fell to her shoulders. One hand was on her right hip. At first, she looked as though she'd rehearsed the same attitude he had. Her hand dropped from her hip, his hand left his pocket and the other dropped the file. They stepped forward and fell into each other's arms. He couldn't help himself and he guessed she couldn't either, although he wasn't so sure of that. They stood that way for at least a minute, then he reached under the back of her legs and carried her to the bed. She had gained some weight but was still slight. He laid her on the bed and lay down alongside her. After a while she got up and went into the bathroom. He could hear the water running in the sink. When she came out, she was naked. Jacks stood up and started to undress, she helped, unbuttoning his shirt carefully, smiling now, then she pulled down the bed cover and climbed under the sheet. They both remembered that little room years ago on Hamburger Allee in Frankfurt.

Afterwards they fell asleep, exhausted not only from the lovemaking, but also from the events of the past two days. The telephone woke them. Jacks looked at his watch, it was five o'clock. "Don't answer it," he told her. "It must be my secretary." She went into the bathroom, turned on the shower, came out again and took his hand. They used to shower together in Frankfurt. It was like returning to a previous life, the water pouring down on them as they soaped each other with caressing hands. She giggled when an erection arose as she soaped his penis, then she mumbled something in German that he didn't get, shook her head and let cold water run on it till it subsided.

They were dressed again, sitting across from each other in armchairs, sipping from a bottle of excellent Argentine wine from the minibar, both waiting for the other to begin the conversation they dreaded.

16 Revelation (cont.)

Jacks sighed: "Okay, Anneliese, or Frau Marie, what's going on?" He tried to smile so it wouldn't seem too much like an interrogation, but interrogators smile too.

"Where do you want me to start, Marvin?"

"From the beginning, I guess." The revelation that she and her husband were East German spies posing as refugees when they first met in Frankfurt didn't surprise him. She also said that during their short-lived affair both her husband and their handler knew about it and her mission was to get information from him and, if possible, to turn him, that is, to recruit him as a double agent. She fell in love with him though – an occupational hazard, it seems – and didn't know what to do until the situation resolved itself through instructions from Berlin to go to Hamburg with a new identity, identities that is, for her husband and herself. Jacks interrupted to ask if her marriage was real or part of her cover. She said both, that it was cover, but had to be real in order to be convincing. But that she hadn't even known Cornelius until they were ordered to marry. Her daughter was the fruit of the marriage but, she insisted, she still loved Jacks and even the child had originally been part of the cover. She was in tears now, so Jacks waited for her to recover, or seem to, before asking how Argentina came into the picture.

"It was 1973, when Perón returned to Argentina," she said. "It was chaos here and they – Wolff, the Stasi chief, I mean – wanted us to come and help the leftist groups, you know, the revolution. In Berlin, and Moscow too probably, they thought Argentina might be ripe, probably because Che Guevara was Argentine, I don't know."

"Seems vague," Jacks said.

"Isn't it always? We were also to establish an identity here and eventually emigrate to the United States."

"Ah, and it didn't work?"

"It worked, but they wanted us back in Germany for something else, so we went and then returned to Argentina three years ago."

Jacks was wary, not sure why she was telling him all this, or even if it was the truth; but he wanted to believe her. If you can't believe the one you love, you can't believe anyone. "With the same identity?" he asked.

"Yes, we still had our National Identity Cards, which never expire."

"And the same mission?"

"Essentially yes, but now I know that the revolution cannot succeed here, so I at least help people who are wanted by the police and armed forces escape, get out of the country."

She foraged in her handbag and came up with a crumpled package of local cigarettes, black tobacco. Jacks checked his pocket for a lighter but couldn't find it. She found a box of matches in the bag, offered him a cigarette, which he declined, and lit up. She held the cigarette as she always had, between her thumb and index finger, like a dubious insect.

"You mean the ERP people?" ERP meant *Ejército Revolucionario del Pueblo*, a Marxist group which had started by hijacking trucks carrying food and clothing and distributing it to the poor. Then they decided they needed money, so robbed banks and kidnapped people for ransom. They also killed some generals, which was definitely a no-no. After the military coup the generals began a campaign to wipe out all resistance. They didn't bother with concentration camps, they just murdered everyone even suspected of having a connection with the insurgents. This finally caused a reverse migration to Europe, mostly to Spain and Italy, not only of insurgents and their friends, but also journalists, scientists, teachers, psychologists, even some Catholic priests after six of their colleagues were murdered and they realized that the Church hierarchy not only would do nothing to defend them but acquiesced in the state terror. As Anneliese and Jacks sat talking in the Sheraton, that cleansing "proceso," as they called it, was in full swing.

"For example, yes," she said, "the ERP people."

"That's very dangerous, Anne ... er ... what *is* your name, by the way?"

"Call me Marie so you won't slip when someone is around. And I know it's dangerous, yes, I know."

"But your real name?"

"Judith. Judith Baumgartner."

"Oh." A long pause while Jacks searched in his pocket for his pipe and tobacco and tried to think of what to say next. She beat him to it.

"What about you, Marvin? You are Marvin, aren't you?"

"Yes, yes I am."

"Really not married?"

"Well, legally yes, still, but it's over, she's in Switzerland."

"Swiss?"

"No, Argentine, it's a long story."

"Any children?"

"No."

She sighed as if relieved by one complication less. Then: "We're quite safe though. My husband's name is Clement now, a native Argentine who emigrated to Germany as a very young child and has now returned with his German bride. Very romantic, but all in order, papers and everything – and it explains his accent. He even learned to be a cook.

"You're not as safe as you think, Judith." He used her name consciously; he had to have something real. She didn't object.

"What do you mean?"

"Yesterday ... no, back in Frankfurt I was also spying on you. They suspected you, at least one sergeant did, so I was assigned to accidentally meet you off duty and try to find out." He thought she'd be shocked, but she only blew a smoke ring and said, smiling, "I knew."

"You mean you guessed."

"In this game guessing is as good as knowing, darling. You were very obvious."

"But I really fell in love with you," he protested.

"I knew that, too. Give me your hand." She held it in both of hers and kissed it. "I fell in love with you, too, Marvin, and I've never loved anyone else." Their knees were touching, and she kissed his hand again. Tears came to his eyes, but he held them back. He didn't know what to do, or even to believe her, that was the worst part.

"I didn't tell them about the room on Hamburger Allee though ... but then you disappeared."

"Yes, we were ordered to Hamburg to support the *Rote Armee Faktion*, but I don't want to talk about that. I couldn't tell you I was a spy, it was impossible, but I was so sorry."

"Just one more thing, Judith."

"Yes, my love?"

"In San Francisco, Olga, was that you?"

She smiled. "Yes, I hope you liked my phony Russian accent. It was actually a training mission. I was supposed to recruit people to our side. The French sailor was a fool and easy, but meaningless. But you would have been a feather in my cap even if you didn't turn. I expected you to call. When you didn't, I thought you suspected something."

"No, I was pretty drunk and lost the paper your number was on." They laughed together. "I was very disappointed. I went to Frisco the next weekend but couldn't even find that bar."

"A stroke of luck for both of us, I think." She said, seriously.

At that moment Jacks made up his mind to believe her, a leap of faith.

"Okay, anyway a guy from the CIA contacted me yesterday." Her eyes opened wider, very attentive now. "They suspect you, Judith."

"But how?"

"Freddy Hussein, they seem to know a lot about him, and they've been following him. They saw me go with him to your restaurant the other day and they know he's been there often."

"Damn! I knew that guy was trouble, a complete idiot."

"Yeah, well, that's why they talked to me, want me to find out what he – and you – are up to. It's dangerous, Judith, all they have to do is tip off the Argentine S.I.D.E., who know how to get everything you know from you, and then 'disappear' you afterwards."

She sat there staring at her hands which rested between her legs. Finally, "I know," she said, "but I don't know what to do."

"I've been thinking about it," Jacks said," and I see two possibilities."

Her eyes asked him what they were.

"Go over to the CIA, ask for protection in exchange for information. I could arrange that." She didn't say anything, waiting for the second choice.

"Or," he said, "leave the country, escape."

She smiled. "They both sound so easy, Marvin, but I don't think they are."

"I didn't say they'd be easy, but let's examine them anyway. First, the CIA ..."

"They would certainly want more than information," she said, without the smile. "They'd want me to be a double agent, and I'm not prepared to do that – or do you think I should? Never mind. And I wouldn't want to give them information either. I'm not a traitor, Marvin."

"This is different, Judith. You must know by now that the German Democratic Republic is a corrupt satellite of the Soviet Union, and sooner or later it's going down the drain. Thousands have defected to the west. Why not you?"

"I ... I don't know. I'm not just someone, one of the thousands, I'm a professional spy for God's sake, Marvin."

"Okay, let's just look at the second alternative for a moment."

"Escape? Where would I go? And Micaela?"

"Micaela?"

"My daughter."

"Oh, well, she'd go with you of course, to Mexico and finally across the border to the States – for example. There are other possibilities I'm sure."

"They'd find me, Marvin. I know too much."

"Not if the CIA gives you a new identity and takes care of you there. I can talk to them, Judith, say you definitely won't be a double agent, but you'll tell them all you know in exchange for getting out, new identity and protection. I can at least ask."

She smiled at his naiveté, which wasn't really that, just grasping at straws. "That would be telling them what I am. They may suspect now, but they don't know."

He took one of her cigarettes, started to light it, threw it down and tried to relight his pipe. She leaned forward and took his hand. "Let me think, *Liebling*, I need to think. Now I must go. Don't call or come to the restaurant. I'll contact you. She stood up. *Ich liebe dich, Marvin.*"

"I love you too, Judith, and ..." She held her hand up, palm out like a policeman directing traffic, and said, "Don't get up."

"The room is still available," he said. "Can you come back?" She shook her head, turned and walked out the door.

He waited until the next morning to pay the hotel bill, pretending that Ms. Albrecht of IATA had stayed the night.

17 S.I.D.E. Comes Aboard

The next morning Marvin Jacks received a telex from his boss Ian Payne telling him to go to Geneva right away for an important meeting. Judith had said not to call her, that she'd contact him. She was right of course, so all he could do was tell his secretary that if Ms Alemán called to tell her that he had to leave on a business trip and would be back in a few days.

When he did return Amalia gave him a list of calls: airline managers mostly, including Armstrong of Panam, a few personal ones, but no Alemán. Maybe she didn't identify herself. He asked Amalia if anyone had called without giving their name. His secretary thought a moment, then said no, not that she could remember. "Only a guy name of Rodriguez who wouldn't say what he wanted. Said he'd call back. Do you want me to call anyone now, Marvin?" He shook his head. "Dictation?" He always dictated a report on his return from trips. He shook his head again, went into his office and when he was about to close the door she asked, *"mate cocido?"* – the bitter tea she knew Marvin liked. "Yes, thanks, Amalia."

There was a knock on the door – three times, with determination. "I'll go," Jacks said. He looked through the peephole, one was careful those days because of the kidnappings. A short man stood in the hall in a rumpled suit under an open trench coat, cigarette dangling from his lips a la Bogart, only lacking the fedora. He seemed to be alone. "Sí?" Jacks called through an intercom. The man looked around for a microphone. "Just speak up, I'll hear you," Jacks said. The man took a wallet from his breast pocket, flipped it open and held it up to the peephole. "Rodriguez, S.I.D.E." The Argentine state intelligence service. Jacks swore to himself and opened the door. "Sr. Hacks?" the man asked. He actually looked a little like Bogart, but his voice was more Peter Lorre.

"Yes. What can I do for you?"

"May I come in? I'd like to ask you some questions."

Once in Jacks' office, he closed the door, much to Amalia's disappointment.

"You are an investigator for the IATA?" Rodriguez said something he obviously already knew.

"Yes," Jacks replied, "And you are one for the S.I.D.E.?"

"Yes," Rodriguez smiled, "so in a way we are colleagues, except for pay scale."

Jacks smiled back, doubting that Rodriguez depended on his salary alone. "Would you like a mate cocido?

"Yes, thank you."

"Amalia, two mate cocidos," Jacks called out, letting Rodriguez know that the door was thin.

"Sí, señor," she called back.

"You are of course wondering why I am here, Mr. Hacks." Jacks often had visits from police detectives investigating travel agency rip-offs or airline security, but this was the first time a S.I.D.E investigator had wanted to see him, so he was curious – and nervous. During the course of the past month, he had become involved with STASI, CIA. and now S.I.D.E. He hoped that they weren't all connected, but feared they were. Amalia came in with two cups of mate cocido on a tray with a sugar bowl and a few cookies. The water must have been already hot, Jacks thought. When she left, leaving the door open, Rodriguez frowned and whispered, "This is very confidential, Sr. Hacks." Jacks nodded. He called Amalia who appeared immediately in the doorway hoping to get in on the dirt. "Sí, señor?" the "señor" being for Rodriguez's benefit.

"I forgot about your mother being sick. You can take the rest of the day off."

"But ..." Jack was glaring at her with his chin high. "*Muy bien, gracias,*" with acid in the last word. She didn't exactly slam the door behind her, just closed it with more force than necessary. They were silent until they heard the outside door close, with a definite slam.

"Thank you," Rodriguez said and sipped from his cup. "I don't wish to take up more of your time than is necessary, Sr. Hacks. So can you please tell me if you know a Karl-Heinz and Marie Clement?"

Jacks thought a moment, then shook his head. "No, I don't think so."

"They are the owners of a restaurant, Die Glocke, in the town of Florida."

"Oh yes," Jacks said with a slight smile, remembering his anti-interrogation techniques, which essentially consisted in remaining calm, "I do know them slightly but didn't know that name."

"You live in Florida, isn't that right?"

"Yes."

"And you have been to the restaurant?"

"Yes, but only once."

"Isn't that unusual?"

"No, you see basically I only sleep in Florida. I eat in the city."

He smiled. "Very understandable. But your name and number is listed in their telephone book, so we thought you might know them better."

"I gave Frau Marie my card when she was introduced to me, something I am too much in the habit of doing I'm afraid."

"Who introduced you?"

"Freddy Hussein. He invited me for lunch there."

"Why did he invite you for lunch?"

"He's in the airline business. Airline managers often invite me for lunch. "

"How well do you know him?"

"Not well at all."

"I see you smoke a pipe, Sr. Hacks." He was looking at Jacks' row of pipes on his desk. "Do you mind if I smoke?"

"Not at all." Jacks took one of the pipes from the rack and went through the tobacco filling ritual while Rodriguez lit a cigarette.

"I tried to switch to a pipe once, but couldn't get used to it," Rodriguez said.

"It takes a while." Get on with it, you bastard, Jacks thought.

Rodriguez blew a noxious cloud of smoke from his blacks into the room and Jacks puffed mightily to cover the smell.

"We suspect that they are spies," Rodriguez said suddenly, and Jacks had to concentrate to show the right mix of surprise and innocence.

"Who?"

"We know that Hussein is a spy, for anyone who will pay him, including us. Mr. And Mrs. Clement – Frau Marie, you know? – we suspect that they are East German spies."

"East German spies – in Argentina?"

"Oh yes, we have all kinds of spies here, Czech, Polish, British, American and etcetera and etcetera, so why not East German as well?" Despite his Bogart appearance, this guy was a Peter Lorre type to the bones, complete with an oily smile. Jacks smiled back as though appreciating the joke.

"What did you and Frau Marie talk about?"

"Nothing much. Let me think. (pause) She told me they'd been in Argentina twice, from Hamburg I think, that the restaurant was doing well, that kind of thing."

"And the husband?"

"No, we shook hands, and he went back to the kitchen."

"That's all?"

"I think so, yes, that's all."

Rodriguez squeezed his nose, scratched an eyebrow and pulled an earlobe in classic interrogator coming-to-the-point mode. "Sr. Hacks, your country and mine are allies in the fight against communism, and it is for that reason that I am sure you will cooperate with us here on our battlefield." He waited for Jacks' reaction.

"Of course – and I've already told you all I know."

"Yes, but we would like you to take advantage of your contacts with these people in order to find out more."

"Sr. Rodriguez," Jacks began, throwing caution to the wind, "I dislike communism as much as you do, but I also dislike military dictatorships, and ..."

"But Señor, we are in complete agreement," Rodriguez said, smiling. "I also dislike dictatorships – except when they are necessary, when there is no other choice. And we have no other choice if we don't want our country to be taken over by the Bolsheviks, and then the domino effect of the rest of the Latin American countries falling one after the other. You see that, don't you?"

"Let's just say I understand the argument," Jacks replied, not wanting to get into a debate he had already had with many Argentines and Americans – especially not with a guy who could "disappear" people at will.

"Good," Rodriguez said dryly, "at least that. But back to our spies – or should I say "alleged" spies. You see, for you alleged means nothing has been proven yet, but for us alleged is enough. We could simply arrest them and find out most of what we want using ... mmm ... other methods? Yes, we could do that, as some of my colleagues are recommending, strongly. But I? Well, I prefer more subtle methods. I would like to find out more before the trail gets cold, which is what would happen if we arrested them now. And you can help me win the argument with my less subtle comrades. Do you follow me?"

Jacks stood, walked to the window and opened it wide to let some smoke out of the room. "Yes," he said. Rodriguez, professional interrogator, understood and waited. Jacks' thoughts went something like this: If I agree now it will seem as though I want to protect them, or at least Frau Marie and if I hardly know her why would I care? Why would I want to do that? So, he breathed deeply at the window, then returned to his chair and looked at Rodriguez.

"So, what do you say?" Rodriguez asked.

"You can all go to hell for all I care," Jacks said as calmly as he could.

Rodriguez smiled. He seemed to really enjoy the little cat and mouse game. He had tried one avenue, but the mouse was more slippery than he thought. So, he would fall back on a more effective trap. "I have no doubt that we are all in grave danger of going there, Señor, but I have faith, you see. You are not a Christian, I assume?"

Jacks knew that by "Christian," he meant Roman Catholic, and he said, "No, but I was once."

"Once a Christian, always a Christian."

"You mean Catholic."

"Of course, yes, thank you for correcting me: Catholic. You see, I hope to avoid hell no matter how much time I must spend in purgatory, for I know my goal is true and the same as the Mother Church's."

God, thought Jacks, the man is mad. "Your confessor told you so?"

"As a matter of fact, yes. But I would have continued on the same path whatever he told me."

"Or changed confessors."

Rodriguez laughed out loud. "Yes, yes, I'm so glad to talk about such things with a man who has a sense of humor." He sighed. "Unfortunately, we haven't time to go more deeply into such things, even if they are extremely important. Now, my apostate friend, please understand that we can make things difficult for you here."

A direct threat, Jacks thought. Better. And for the first time it occurred to him to wonder if Armstrong had something to do with this visit.

"Really," he said. "How?"

"Never mind how," Rodriguez said. "Trust me, we can."

They sat there for at least a minute smiling idiotically at each other. Rodriguez thinking that Jacks' was imagining the terrible things they could do to him. Jacks, however, thinking, hoping, that he was bluffing. Jacks was, after all, a U.S. citizen, an ally with connections to his embassy and the representative of an important international organization of which Argentina's national airline was a member. But he knew that there were certain unimaginably horrible things they could do to Judith Baumgartner if they discovered her real identity and chose to take that avenue.

"Let me think about it," he said, finally.

Rodriguez stood, still grinning, shook Jacks' hand, said, *"Gracias por el mate cocido,"* and left.

Jacks' first impulse was to phone Armstrong, but then he thought the bastards might have his phone tapped, so he decided to take the subway for the two stops to Panam's office. He bought a subway token for twenty centavos but put it in his pocket and decided to walk. It would give him time to think. He made his way down Avenida Santa Fe in bright autumn sunshine. A visitor who didn't keep up with the news and who walked down that luxurious shopping street could never know that Argentina was run by a brutal military dictatorship and that the city of Buenos Aires was surrounded by a ring of shanty towns called *villa miserias.* When he reached Avenida Corrientes, a main traffic artery full of buses belching clouds of exhaust smoke and honking taxis, he turned right towards the obelisk at the Plaza de la República. He didn't notice anything around him, for he was thinking of what he would say to Armstrong. He had to contain his anger first of all because he wasn't sure that Armstrong was behind the S.I.D.E. guy's visit and also because it wouldn't do any good. He was also more fearful than ever about Judith's safety. Now he could tell her that not only CIA, but also the S.I.D.E. was on her trail and she had to move – and quickly. Not that easy because her phone was certainly tapped. He turned left automatically at the Plaza de la República when he reached the obelisk, walked down Diagonal Norte dodging pedestrians, crossed it and stepped into the Panam building.

"Oh, hello, Mr. Jacks," Armstrong's secretary said in perfect Anglo-Argentine English. "How are you today?" Jacks wondered if she was also CIA; after all, it would be hard to keep secrets from a personal secretary, better to recruit her.

"Fine, Beatríz, thanks." Jacks knew the value of being on good terms with secretaries. They could open or close doors. "Gotta see John."

"He's in a meeting right now, Mr. Jacks," she said apologetically. "You didn't have an appointment, did you? We've been trying to contact you."

"With whom?"

"Sorry?"

"Who's he meeting with?"

"The sales manager."

"Tell him I'm here and I have to speak with him urgently."

"Well ..." She frowned; all an act Jacks knew.

"Please, Bea."

She smiled. "All right, Mr. Marvin Jacks." She swiveled towards him revealing slender unstockinged legs and a peek at her panties under a miniskirt, stood and walked into the boss's office. A minute later she came out, followed by the sales manager, a harassed-looking guy whose name Jacks had forgotten, who shook Jacks' hand, gratefully it seemed, because he got him out of Armstrong's clutches.

"You can go in now, Mr. Jacks," the secretary said, but he had already walked past her into the inner sanctum.

"Hi, Marvin," Armstrong began, "You know, airline seats are the hardest things in the world to sell. They're intangibles for god's sake. Maybe I should go into the used car business. Sit down, what can I do for you?"

"Let's go downstairs for a coffee," Jacks said.

"What? Why? We have better coffee here … oh, I getcha. Don't worry, pal, this place is debugged, completely and forever. So, sit down and relax. He pushed the intercom button: "Bea, bring us two coffees, the Colombian stuff."

Jacks remained standing. "A S.I.D.E. guy came to see me." He watched Armstrong's reaction, which consisted of a raising of eyebrows.

"No kidding," he said. "What the fuck do they want? Sit the hell down, will you. You're making me nervous."

Jacks sat in an armchair across from Armstrong in the VIP corner and frowned at him. "They want me to work for them, find out about Frau Marie."

"Jeez, that's interesting," Armstrong said. "Tell me more."

"When I demurred, he threatened me."

"Really? How?"

"That's what I asked him. He said I should trust him they could do it."

"Well …"

"I trust him," Jacks said. "And I want to know if you had anything to do with it."

"Me?" – The secretary walked in without knocking, carrying a tray with two cups of aromatic Colombian coffee, cream, sugar, the works.

She set it down on the table between them. "Thank you, Bea," Armstrong said with a smile. You could cut the silence until she left. "Why would I do something like that, Marvin?"

"You want me to do the same thing. Maybe this is a less than subtle way of saying I'm better off working for you than for them."

"What exactly do you mean by 'demurred'?" Armstrong asked.

"I said I didn't like dictatorships."

"Nice. Did you outright refuse?"

"I said I'd think about it."

"Same answer you gave me. Okay, Marvin, I categorically deny having had anything to do with this. Furthermore ..."

"I'm asking you yes or no, John, goddammit. I'm not interested in categorical denials."

Armstrong stared at him a moment, then said, "No, definitely not, Marvin. I wouldn't do that, and I didn't. That good enough for you?"

"Are you the boss here?"

"What do you mean – the boss?"

"Of the CIA in Argentina is what I mean."

"There's a Station Chief at the embassy of course. He wouldn't do it, Marvin." He paused and looked at the tray. "Our coffee's getting cold. Cream and sugar?"

"No."

Armstrong poured, half-filled his own cup with sugar, then said, "Well, maybe he would, but not without consulting me."

"Get them off my back, John," Jacks said as calmly as he could.

"We didn't put them there, Marvin … but don't worry, we'll talk to them. What's the guy's name?"

"Rodriguez, here's his card."

"I'll tell them you're working for us then?"

"Don't fuck with me, John."

"I have to tell them something. Look, Marvin, we didn't set it up, but it just turned out that way. We work with those bastards, sure, we have no choice, but that doesn't mean we like them, or that they like us. So, the only way we can convince them is to say that you're already on the case – for us."

Jacks wasn't surprised at this turn of events; in fact he expected it. It was, after all, logical, whether the CIA was behind the S.I.D.E. intervention or not. All he needed now was for the KGB to show up.

"All right, John," he said, trying to sound resigned. "What do you want me to do?"

"That's my man!" Armstrong said. "We're gonna drink to that." He jumped up and pushed the intercom on his desk.

"Yes, sir," his secretary answered,

"Bring in a small bottle of champagne – the French."

They sat in silence waiting for the toast. Jacks filled his pipe. When the champagne arrived a minute later, already opened with a white towel around it, Armstrong poured, handed a glass to Jacks and said, "To you Marvin; you won't be sorry."

Jacks sipped first, then downed the champagne in one gulp. "So, what do you want me to do?"

"Suck up to Frau Marie, you've already got one foot in the door. Find out what they're up to, who they really are, her and her husband I mean."

"And you'll call off the Argentines, the S.I.D.E.?

"Right, I'll take care of that right away, don't want them fucking things up."

"You better call them off Frau Marie and hubby as well," Jacks said. "I can't very well find out anything if they're hanging by their toes in some clandestine torture cell."

"Good point, not as easily done, but good point. This is good stuff, isn't it. The French may be assholes, but they sure know how to make champagne." Armstrong looked at his watch. "How about lunch, Marvin?"

"No thanks, John. I have a week's backlog of work back at the office."

18 Surveillance

But Jacks didn't go back to his office. It was almost lunch time, and he knew where he was going to eat. They – the CIA and the S.I.D.E. – were watching Die Glocke, but now that he was, theoretically at least, working for them both, one directly the other indirectly, there was good reason for him to go there. Time was of the essence, he had to warn Anneliese … Judith … Marie. He asked Armstrong's secretary if he could use her phone. She, thinking it was an excuse to flirt with her, said of course he could, and pointed to the phone instead of pushing it across the desk to him, so he had to walk around and stand next to her while he dialed. She pressed her naked thigh into his and bent over to look at some papers in order to reveal an ample cleavage.

Frau Marie answered. "I'd like to reserve a table for lunch today," Jacks said in German, sure she'd recognize his voice and slight accent. Silence. Then, "Under what name?" "Schmidt," Jacks replied, feeling silly. "Jawohl, Herr Schmidt." Jacks hung up the phone slowly, letting his arm touch the secretary's breast. "See you soon, Bea."

"Auf Wiedersehen, Herr Jacks."

Do you speak German?" he asked her.

"No, but I saw The Sound of Music three times," she giggled.

Outside on the street Jacks wondered if he was being followed, not that it mattered now, but he wanted to know. He knew something about surveillance techniques from his M.I. training. There are several levels: if you want the target to know he's being watched you stay very close on his tail, and one person can do it; if you prefer that he not know, but it's more important that he not be lost, you stay close but not too close and you need at least two people, one on each side of the street. If you don't want the target to know that he's being tailed you need at least three people, preferably four, to keep changing positions. Jacks also knew something about avoiding surveillance. In Germany he had often gone through the motions but never really knew if he was being followed. The Stasi, Germans in Germany, were experts. The M. I. people, like him, were amateurs, but losing a tail, called counter-surveillance, was much easier than doing the tailing. Like so much else in life, negation was the easy way.

He crossed the wide Diagonal Norte with the traffic light and walked south in the general direction of his office. After a block he came to the subway entrance. He was at the hub of the Buenos Aires subway system where all the lines crossed and downstairs it was like a human beehive. He stopped before a men's clothing store and gazed into the shop window. In the glass's reflection he saw a man directly across the street from him looking into the window of a store, a women's lingerie shop. He was undoubtedly watching Jacks in the reflection. Good. Now Jacks turned his head left in the direction from which he had come. It wouldn't do at all for a tail to stop as well and be identified. No, he would continue walking, pass the target, then turn a corner and wait for the target to pass him. The guy across the street would signal which way the target was going. Jacks kept his head turned left, watching everyone who passed him; he was waiting for everyone a half-block behind him to pass, with one eye on the guy across the street. When he was satisfied that everyone had passed and had time to get a safe distance beyond him, he turned and quickly walked down the steep stairs to the subway. He felt into his pocket for the token he had bought an hour ago but luckily hadn't used. If he'd had to wait in line for a token, they'd have had time to catch up. He pushed through the crowd, inserted the token into the turnstile and walked quickly to the line going north. When he got to the platform, he was again lucky for a train was just pulling in. He boarded it, certain that he'd shaken his followers. He'd be picked up again at Die Glocke, but at least they'd know he was not to be fucked with.

19 Argentine Airlines

He parked in a restricted area a few blocks from the airline's head office. A parking ticket didn't bother him; he only hoped they wouldn't tow away the car. A year previously he had arranged for an intermediary to buy an Argentine Airlines test ticket at a fifty percent discount. Airlines and travel agents may give discounts to win passengers, but fifty percent is impossible unless something more serious is going on. He suspected that the ticket had been stolen, which was the only way he knew for such a large discount to be profitable. But he was mistaken. It turned out that the General, president of the airline, had been supplying his mistress – or mistresses – with free tickets, and one of them had turned such a freebie over to a travel agent for resale. When Jacks discovered this, it presented a problem. If he followed procedure and filed a complaint against the airline and the travel agent, he would have to tell the whole story, step by step, in a sworn affidavit, including the result of his investigation, that the General had simply given the ticket away. He would of course deny everything despite the overwhelming evidence. There would be a huge scandal which could have resulted in Jacks being declared persona non grata in Argentina. In fact, that very thing had happened to an over-zealous colleague in another country.

However, he couldn't simply forget about it, because some people in the airline's accounting department knew that their President had authorized the issuance of the free ticket which, although technically prohibited, was fairly common only when important political or military figures were the beneficiaries, which was far from the case here. Furthermore, he had already spent IATA's money to buy the ticket and it had to be accounted for.

So, he had gone to the General, showed him the evidence and asked if he had an explanation. Santamaría's face got very red, but then he took a Havana cigar from a humidor, offered Jacks one and they smoked in silence while he sweated in thought. Jacks hoped that one option wasn't opening a trap door for him to fall through. Finally, though, the general said that he had obviously made a grave personal mistake and asked Jacks if there was anything he could do for him that would convince him not to proceed. He was offering a bribe, but all Jacks wanted was a way out. He told him he didn't want to embarrass him but didn't see a way out because those other people in his airline knew about the ticket, as did IATA. General Santamaria almost jumped out of his chair and opened a cabinet behind him, selected a bottle of Napoleon cognac, poured for them both and said: "Mr. Hacks, they will be silent; I guarantee it." Jacks believed him. And from that moment on the General owed him.

He got General Santamaría's secretary on the phone, an accomplishment in itself. He identified himself, something she already knew because he had gone through three sub-secretaries to get to her. She told him (naturally) that the General was in a meeting, and asked what the subject of his need to speak to him was. "*De qué asunto es?*" a perennial question in the Spanish language business and political worlds. Jacks told her to please announce to him, that the subject was confidential and extremely urgent. She told him to hold. It seemed like a half-hour but was probably only a few minutes later that General Santamaría came on the line. She probably had to wake him up.

"Yes, Mr. Hacks, how are you and what can I do for you?"

You might think that Jacks should have just gone to his office and barged in. But you would be wrong. That would have been an inexcusable lack of etiquette in dealing with a person of his self-esteem. Furthermore, he wouldn't have gotten past the guards on the ground floor. Jacks told him that he had to see him immediately, that the future of his airline and the nation was at stake. He implied it at least.

"Well, let me see ..." the general began as though looking through his appointments schedule.

"I'm across the street, General, if you'll advise the guards, I can be in your office in two minutes." This was unheard of, but as the fog dissipated from his brain, he was remembering that Jacks knew something which he didn't want anyone else to know. "Bueno," he growled, "make it five," and slammed down the receiver.

Jacks left the public phone booth and sprinted down Avenida Colón. The guards asked for his ID, frisked him and let him ride up to the fifth floor in the elevator, but not alone; one of them accompanied him. They were exceedingly polite, figuring that anyone important enough to be seeing the General must have at least some residual importance. Santamaría kept him waiting fifteen minutes, something important people always do. The waiting calmed Jacks though, and he was prepared to say what he had to say.

General Santamaría sat behind his enormous desk smoking a Havana cigar and wishing that Jacks wasn't there. Jacks told him that the S.I.D.E. had fucked up by arresting Frau Marie and hubby because he was just about to get really top-secret information from her for the CIA that would deal the Commies a blow they wouldn't recover from during that millennium, if ever. Yes, he was undercover CIA. What he didn't mention, but was lurking in the noxious air, was that he still knew about the free tickets the general gave to his girlfriends. He listened pulling on his earlobe and scratching his balls and when Jacks finished, he said, "Those guys (meaning S.I.D.E.) think they own the country," He thought a moment, then added, "Call me in an hour – at this number, from a pay phone." He scribbled a number on a slip of paper and handed it to Jacks. *"Mil gracias, General,"* Jacks mumbled as he backed out half-bowing.

Jacks walked around close to the Plaza de Mayo telephone center during that interminable hour. When he called Santamaría, he said, "Well Señor Hacks, *she's* out, but they wouldn't release the husband, he's a KGB officer. Anyway, they did me the favor. I hope it helps you." Meaning that Jacks owed *him* now. Jacks controlled his elation and assured the general that it would help. Was he glad that her husband hadn't been released? Yes. Did he feel guilty about it? No.

Jacks decided to call from the same phone booth first Die Glocke, then her home, although he doubted that she'd be either place so soon. Then, if there was no answer, he'd go to his house, where she'd be looking for her daughter – and maybe even him. But she answered Die Glocke after the first ring.

"I'd like to make a reservation for tonight," he said in German.

"I'm sorry but we're closed tonight," she answered.

"This is Marvin Jacks." They'd be expecting him to contact her anyway; now they'd have to record the conversation and find someone to translate it, which would cause at least a short delay. "In that case perhaps we could go someplace together for dinner."

"Yes, that would be nice, Herr Jacks."

"But you'll probably want to go home first to change."

"That would be a good idea ... er, do you know where my daughter is?"

"Yes, of course. I'll bring her with me in, say, an hour? Oh, and I thought we might go to the seashore for the weekend. What do you think about that?"

"Yes. Thank you very much."

"Good, then you can pack some things for Micaela and yourself."

"Yes."

"See you in an hour then."

"Yes."

Jacks wanted her to pick up their passports but didn't dare mention it on the phone. He went home, threw a few things in an overnight bag, put his passport in his breast pocket and strapped a 22 pistol around his ankle. If they ever got on an airplane, he'd have to ditch it, but he wouldn't be needing it by then anyway. Then he went to the neighbor's, the Altmann's, to get Micaela. She was sitting at a table in the patio under the grapevines drawing a picture with colored crayons. It was such a peaceful setting that he experienced a tinge of doubt as to whether he should take her away from such safety into the dangerous situation her mother and he were about to face. But it wasn't for him to decide. If Judith wanted to leave her, which he doubted, they could always stop by to drop her off before leaving for good.

"What are you drawing, Mica?" he asked her.

"Hola, Marvin." He hadn't told her his name, she must have asked Frau Altmann, who probably was surprised that she didn't know it. "Don't you see? It's an angel." Indeed, it was.

"Yes, I see, and a beautiful one at that." You'll need him now, he thought, we all will.

"Let's go, we're going to pick up your mamá."

She dropped the crayon and jumped up. "Is she all right?"

"Sure she is. Why do you ask?"

"I don't know, she's been kind of nervous lately."

"Will Micaela be coming back here?" Frau Altmann asked. "She's a delightful child and we're glad to have her."

Jacks hated to lie to that kind lady but had no choice. "Yes," he said, "We're just going to Mar del Plata for the weekend."

Judith was ready to go when they got to her house. "I only packed a few things," she said, still speaking in German, as though it were a continuation of their telephone conversation, probably because of the possibility that her house was bugged, "for the weekend."

"Yes, that's fine." Jacks took a pen from his pocket and signaled for paper, then wrote, in English, *passports?* She nodded.

They left the house smiling – on Jacks' instructions – with Micaela between them. Jacks opened the Mitsubishi's doors and looked to the front, nothing, and behind. There it was – a green Ford Falcon with three goons in it. He had a crazy impulse to take out the 22 and shoot at them. Are they stupid or are they stupid? It was a dead giveaway that they were being followed. Well, maybe they didn't care about that. But that car was the fastest tractor on the road, and he could easily lose it. Now they'd have to head south towards the seashore, instead of north to freedom.

An hour later they were on the highway approaching Chascomus, a sleepy town almost halfway to Mar del Plata. There was, as usual, a lot of Friday afternoon traffic. Jacks gunned the Mitsubishi and left the Falcon way behind. He knew the road well and after a curve he pulled off the highway into Chascomus, went through the town and got onto a secondary road going back north. It was slower and they probably could have gone back to the highway, but why take a chance. What if they'd been seen pulling off and the cops were already watching for them in both directions? There were police controls on the highways, but very few on secondary roads. It took them two hours dodging potholes to get back to Buenos Aires, skirt around it and continue north. It was dark by then and it had already been a long day.

The moon was full though, or almost full. It occurred to Jacks that the moon would be full regardless of what happened to them, whether they escaped and lived happily ever after, or were captured, tortured and killed. That selfish moon doesn't give a damn. Is death like that or is it alive like the sun and the stars? Jacks glanced to his right at his companion, who had been silent for a while, and saw that she was asleep, mouth slightly open, eyelids fluttering. "Frau Marie, Anneliese, Judith – who cares about your name," he whispered, "I love you, and I'll tell you so when you're awake," although he knew he wouldn't, not yet. He wasn't so sure.

They drove all night on flat, bumpy secondary roads, through somnolent towns. Judith took over the wheel for the last two hundred kilometers while Jacks rested his eyes. Micaela had no problem sleeping all night in the back seat. Jacks mentioned how interesting Micaela's school seemed. It was like a cue for Judith. "Yes, I hope there are such schools in America. They are called Steiner or Waldorf schools."

"Is that the gent whose picture hangs on the office wall?"

"Yes, Rudolf Steiner. He was an Austrian philosopher and an initiate. He inaugurated Anthroposophy, which he called spiritual science. And the schools are based on his teachings about the nature of children and how they should be educated."

Marvin Jacks was surprised to hear about spiritual science from a lifelong committed communist. "Hmm, sounds religious, not much like Marxism," he said.

"It's not a religion, but it is kind of religious, but different. I mean it includes reincarnation and karma, things like that."

"Wow, and you believe that stuff?"

She didn't answer for quite a while, probably because she wasn't sure of the answer. When she finally said, "I'm beginning to," Jacks had fallen asleep.

At sunrise they entered the border village of Puerto Iguazú, squeezed onto a narrow tongue of land between Brazil and Paraguay. They stopped and got coffee and stale croissants at a gas station café. While tanking up Jacks asked the attendant for directions to Foz do Iguazú, Brazil.

"You're going to Ciudad del Este, I bet," the attendant said with a toothless smile. Jacks confirmed that they were, although they were going farther than that, to the capital city of Asunción where there was an international airport.

"The immigration assholes probably won't be awake yet, so you can probably get by without a tip. I don't know about the Paraguayan ones though, they're hungrier." Jacks had been to Asunción several times, but never to the infamous "triple frontier" where Argentina, Brazil and Paraguay meet. He knew, however, that Paraguay is the contraband capital of the world, where you can buy anything tax-free and stolen. Most of the new cars stolen in Brazil and Argentina – and they are legion – wind up in Paraguay, where you can buy them at cut-rate prices in police stations. Hundreds of pedestrians and cars cross the bridges every day to shop, and the border police and immigration officials are well paid to keep the traffic moving, not to intercept thieves and smugglers, who are welcome. And it was the perfect place for fugitives, like them, to leave Argentina.

As they approached the bridge over the Rio Paraná to Foz do Iguazú, they saw that the gas station attendant was right – not an immigration soul in sight, so they drove over to Brazil. A half hour later they were at the next bridge over the same river, already full of cars and pedestrians crossing without the immigration people, who were ensconced in the booths slurping mate, paying no attention to them. On the other side was Paraguay. Judith put her hand on his arm and said, "Stop for a minute, Marvin." He pulled over to the side of the road. "They're not stamping passports," she said.

"No, not even looking at them," he replied.

"Yes, but if we intend to fly out of here, we have to show our foreign passports that have no entry stamps."

"We can say we came in here, over the bridge."

"I know something about this place, Marvin," she said. Micaela was listening carefully to this serious conversation. "Remember my real profession." Her real profession, spy, wasn't something she wanted her daughter to hear.

"Go on," he said.

"This bridge is for people who cross with or without documents and who leave the same way at the same place. Air travel is different. They won't let us leave without entry stamps." She paused, waiting for a reaction.

His head was empty. "So, what do we do?"

"We ask the immigration guy to stamp us in, that like most tourists we like stamps in our passports."

Jacks nodded, then said, "But what if they're looking for us?"

"The Paraguayans won't be – not yet at least, I hope."

"Okay, it's worth the risk," he said. "Give me your passports."

She didn't move.

"Judith?"

"I think it would be better if you gave me yours. I'll go in with Micaela. You stay in the car sulking because you think it's silly to waste time for stamps. That's what I'll tell him."

It was obvious that she could charm the pants off any macho, so he nodded approval and handed her his passport. She put a twenty-dollar bill inside it. They drove past the Brazilian immigration booth and stopped at the Paraguayan one fifty yards further on. Judith and Micaela got out of the car and walked in. Jacks watched her smiling at the guard and explaining, then pointing to him with a laugh. He scowled appropriately. The guard had stood up politely. He was talking now and pointing back at the Brazilian side. Judith looked serious. She shook her head and pointed at Jacks again. She picked up the passports and came back to the car clutching Micaela's hand. She leaned into the window.

"He said he couldn't stamp us in without a Brazilian stamp and for that we'd have to have an Argentine one stamping us out," she whispered. "He said we should go back and get the Brazilian and Argentine stamps first. I said you were already angry, and I didn't want to infuriate you, but that I'd ask you."

Jacks' brain started working again. "I don't think it's a good idea."

"Nor do I."

"Get in and let's get out of here."

Judith turned back to the guard, shook her head, shrugged her shoulders and got back into the car with Micaela.

"Have a good visit to Paraguay," the guard called out, happy to have earned twenty bucks for nothing. After she and Micaela were in the car Jacks drove off after wiping the sweat off his hands on his trousers.

"It's suspicious," he said.

"Yes, but he's an idiot."

"But what do we do now without entry stamps?"

"I know a place in Asunción where we can get passports," she said calmly.

"With different names? Great!" Jacks said, thinking that the Paraguayan airport police, also servants of a dictatorship, would be more efficient and might already have their names.

Following Judith's directions, Jacks drove to a slum section of Asunción and stopped at what looked like an oversized box made of rusty corrugated tin. They got out of the car and Micaela held her mother's hand as they walked into the box without knocking. A skinny guy was working on a lathe so didn't hear them come in until they were almost past him. Then he turned off the lathe, stepped in front of Judith, who was in the lead, and said "Señora?"

"We're going to see Agusto," she said.

"Ah, is he expecting you?"

"No, just tell him that Marie from Buenos Aires is here."

"Marie who?"

"Tell him," she replied with an authority that surprised both the skinny guy and Jacks. He turned and walked to the far end of the box, about ten yards away, and knocked – two shorts and a long – and entered. They waited two minutes and the door opened and Agusto came out with a big smile on his fat face. He was wearing a tie and jacket, which he had probably just put on because the shirt under it was soaked with sweat, while the jacket was fresh.

"Señora Marie!" he gushed in Spanish, "such a pleasure to see you again." He took her hand and kissed it, must have seen that in a movie.

He patted Micaela's head, looked at Jacks, then inquiringly at Judith. "*Un amigo,*" she said.

"Ah. Well, please come into my den, said the fly to the spider." He laughed alone at his own joke and led the way back to the den, a luxuriously appointed office in fact. He sat behind an oak desk and motioned for them to sit. Judith remained standing, so Jacks did as well.

"We need three passports, Agusto," she said, "pronto!"

His smile vanished. Business. "I see. For you three?"

"Yes."

"When?"

"Yesterday."

"Any particular nationality?

"What do you have?"

"Paraguayan, of course, then ... let me think ... German?"

"German will do."

"I don't have a child's passport though." Silence. So, they were stolen passports and all he changed were the photographs. "But I may be able to get one. Wait." He picked up his phone and pressed a button on the console, then spoke in a language Jacks guessed was Arabic. It took quite a while, but when he hung up, he smiled his cheesy smile and said, "*No hay problema.*"

"When will they be ready?" Judith asked.

"After the photos, about an hour. You realize of course that the child's passport will cost a bit more because ..."

"The same price as always, Agusto, if you want to keep dealing with us." Cold – she really didn't like this guy, which was easy to understand.

Agusto scowled, but said, "I will make the sacrifice for a lady." He stood up with some effort and pulled back a curtain at one side of the office. "You first, young lady," he said to Micaela, who looked at her mother. Judith nodded and the child stood against a cream-colored plaque against the wall. Agusto snapped her picture and then the others.

"Deliver them to us at the airport," Judith said, forcing a smile. "We'll pay the messenger. He'll know us by the photos."

"As you wish, Señora Marie," Augusto said. "Oh, by the way, I have the new passports here for your two friends, Barkarian and Wilson." He opened a drawer in his desk and took out an envelope. "Do you want to take them with you, or shall I send them?"

"Send them the usual way," Judith said.

"Why don't we take them with us?" Jacks said in German. "It's faster and safer." Agusto may or may not have understood him, but in any case, he sounded like a boss from East Germany, he hoped.

She looked at him, surprised, and said, "Ja, natürlich." Jacks held out his hand to Agusto. He looked at Judith, who nodded, and he gave Jacks the envelope.

While they were driving to the airport, she asked, "Why do you want us to take those passports?"

"Who are they?" he asked.

"Couriers, of no importance."

"We may be able to use them, you never know."

"How much will the passports cost?" Jacks asked her once they got to the airport and saw that there was a Lineas Aéreas Paraguayas flight leaving in two hours for Miami.

"A thousand dollars apiece."

He whistled. "Do we have that much?"

"Maybe, but I have no intention of paying that bastard Agusto that much."

"How will we get the passports then?

"You'll see, come on."

She went to the currency exchange booth and changed a hundred-dollar bill for small denominations, mostly singles. She bought a large envelope, put hundreds at both ends and singles and fives between them and sealed the envelope with strong glue.

"Won't the messenger check?" Jacks asked her.

"I don't think so. We'll soon see."

He didn't. It was a kid who came on a motorbike. They were sitting near the entrance, so he spotted them right away. "Señora María?" he asked.

"Judith held out her hand and the boy put an envelope into it. She handed him the other envelope and a ten-dollar bill. "For you," she said. "*Gracias, señora*," he said smiling, put the envelope in his backpack and sped off. They looked at the passports. Judith and Jacks were, Herr and Frau Müller, and Micaela was Inge Schulz.

Judith looked at Jacks. "*Mein Gott*, your passport name is different from your credit card name."

Jacks smiled. "*No hay problema*." He took the passports and strolled over to the L.A.P. ticket counter. After waiting for the ticket agent to finish with a passenger, he handed her the three passports and his credit card. "I want tickets for these three passengers, Miami, one-way, open." She would have to think he was some kind of unofficial travel agent and there was no law against buying tickets for clients. She made an imprint of the credit card, wrote out the tickets (L.A.P. couldn't afford machines, apparently), he signed and said, "Oh, what's the phone number of reservations again?"

"I can make the reservations for you," she said.

"Yes, but this is for future reference, I'm travelling too, and forgot my address book." She wrote the number on a slip of paper. "Gracias," he said. "*Gracias a usted, señor.*"

He strolled over to the telephone booths, which were all occupied. He waited. Finally, a woman came out of one wiping her eyes. He dialed the number the clerk had given him and asked for three seats on the flight leaving in one hour for Miami. She asked if they could make it to the airport in time. Yes, he said, we're very close. Reservations confirmed. He beckoned Judith and Micaela over and they checked in for the flight. The agent checked her computer, revalidated their tickets and asked about baggage. Only carry-on, Jacks said. Unusual, but so what. "Let's get through immigration before Agusto comes looking for us," he said to Judith.

20 The Defector

... We will be arriving at Buenos Aires International airport in approximately two and a half hours," the intercom on the old Boeing 707 blared almost unintelligibly in Spanish and English. Jacks' heart jumped and he pressed the overhead button for the flight attendant. There were no three seats together available, so Judith and Micaela were seated a few rows ahead of him. Judith was speaking to her daughter and didn't seem to have paid attention to the announcement.

"I thought this flight was going to Miami," Jacks told the flight attendant who was holding onto the overhead baggage rack as she leaned down to hear him.

"We're stopping in Buenos Aires first, señor," she shouted into his ear, "to pick up passengers." And she scuttled down the aisle to other passengers who probably had the same question. Of course, Jacks thought, L.A.P. didn't have enough passengers from Paraguay directly to Miami, so they took a long detour in the opposite direction to pick up passengers in Argentina, where they sold tickets at hefty discounts. He'd forgotten about that.

He knelt alongside Judith and told her that they would be landing in Buenos Aires, but would be in transit, so no problem. Her eyes opened wide as this sunk in, then she just shook her head and sighed, so he went back to his seat.

The transit area at Ezeiza, Buenos Aires's international airport, was chaotic. Hundreds of British passengers were milling around looking nervously at their watches, yelling at their kids to sit still, don't get lost, conferring with each other in whispers. Judith, Micaela and Jacks sat facing the window looking out to the runways so their faces couldn't be seen by passers-by. Refueling would take an hour. An elderly English woman passed in front of them, stopped to look out the window then turned to Jacks, apparently mistaking him for a compatriot and said, "I wonder what's delaying it. Have you heard anything?"

"About what?"

"Do you mean you haven't heard?"

"I guess not."

"The Argies have invaded the Falkland Islands. Can you imagine? We're tourists. They said we can leave, but the British Airways airplane should have been here an hour ago." She put her hand over her mouth. "Oh! You're not Argentineans, are you?"

"No," Jacks said to her immense relief.

An immaculately dressed man about her own age who had been listening from the row behind them came forward and approached her. In accented English he said, "Madam, I *am* an Argentinean and I assure you that we have nothing against you, and you have nothing to worry about. When this terrible nonsense is over, I do hope you will visit us once again. You will be most welcome." He bowed slightly and walked away. The woman, astonished, scurried back to her group with the news.

A few minutes later a man crossed Jack's view and sat next to him. Jacks didn't look at him until he spoke sotto-voce, in English, American accent.

"Hi, Marvin, or should I say Lt. Jacks, retired." After Jacks looked at his profile it took a moment for recognition. He faced forward again and in the same tone said, "Master Sergeant Jack Quinn I presume – without the stripes. What a coincidence."

"I don't believe in coincidences, Jacks; didn't I ever tell you that?"

"Yes, and I'm beginning to agree. So why are we meeting again in this unlikely place?" He was keeping up the tough guy chatter, but his palms were sweating.

"I'm looking for a guy with your name who fits your description to a T, accompanied by a woman and a child who look like the two subjects on your right." Micaela was next to Jacks, asleep with her head in Judith's lap, who couldn't hear their conversation.

"Doesn't sound like a coincidence then," Jacks said.

"Nope."

"Let me guess. CIA?"

"Good guess. Station chief, Rio."

"This is Buenos Aires."

"Also, me. When I got the request to advise all Brazilian entry points to pick up your little family and you on sight, I decided to come on down and look myself, since I can identify you. Our Argentine colleagues are still checking the roads, but I happen to know that you're a frequent flyer."

"So, you've finally made it to the officer class," Jacks said.

Quinn turned his head and looked at Jacks, "You're not makin' a very good impression, Marvin. And I think you'll want to, under the circumstances. Goin' to Miami?"

"Yes, obviously, I hope."

"And then."

"She's defecting, Jack."

"To you?" Quinn growled. "Who the fuck are you?"

"No, to you."

He laughed. "Good one."

"No, I mean it, I'm really glad to see you."

"I should turn you, them that is, over to our friends here, and get them later when it's our turn."

"S.I.D.E.?" You mean you'll get what's left. Give us a break, Jack."

"How'd you get out of Asunción? They're looking for you too."

"I promise we'll go straight to the CIA in Miami. In fact, you can give us the address."

"Seems your girlfriend's important, Marvin, runs the East German covert operation in Latin America."

"Not her husband?

"Her! the hubby's a hit man. You seem to be attracted to female spies. I remember something similar happening in Germany way back then."

"It's the same one, Jack."

Quinn looked over at Judith. "No shit? See what I mean? No coincidences."

"Give us a break, Jack."

"You got no problem," he said. "Just a stupid American bystander."

"It's more complicated than that."

"Okay, let's have it."

"We're travelling with false documents."

Quinn nodded. "So that's how you got out of Paraguay."

Jacks reached into his carry-on and pulled out the envelope the Paraguayan forger had given him. "That's right, and here are forged passports for two East German couriers, with their address in Madrid. And in a minute, I'll give you the name and address of the forger in Asunción." Judith was tapping on her armrest nervously. Quinn glanced at the passports, put them in his pocket, and said, "Let's change seats." They switched seats and Quinn said to Judith, in German, "Are you defecting to the United States of America?" She didn't bother to look at Jacks for confirmation, just said, "*Jawohl.*"

"Trust me, Quinn," Jacks said, "we'll check in at the CIA on arrival."

"I trust you, Marvin, so much so that I'm gonna leave you alone here for a few minutes while I go downstairs to buy a ticket on this flight. Here's my card. If anyone bothers you – this place is crawling with S.I.D.E. looking for the horde of British spies they're imagining – tell them you're waiting for me." He stood up and started to walk away, then stopped and sat again on Jack's side away from Judith. "Are you sticking with her, I mean for good?"

"I guess so," an answer that surprised even Jacks by its lack of enthusiasm.

During the long flight to Miami Marvin Jacks had another revelation. He had been in love with Anneliese Cornelius a long time ago, who wasn't real then, and was even less real now as Frau Marie Clement. He didn't know her very well and wasn't sure if he wanted to know Judith Baumgartner, super spy, all that well either. Oh, he'd stick with her all right, through her CIA interrogation hell, which would be a hell of a lot more comfortable than a S.I.D.E. one. A defector is treated much better than a captured spy; one is a repentant friend and the other a recalcitrant enemy. He was confident that his old buddy, ex-Master Sergeant Jack Quinn, would see to it that she was a defector. Although he said a few words to her and she responded with only one, the gleam in his eye when he looked at her indicated that he would much prefer to have her as a friend. She'd have a secret identity in the U.S. for a while, until the German Democratic Republic and its obscene Berlin Wall collapsed, which wasn't so far in the future, Jacks assumed, and then she'd want to go back to Germany, which wasn't his cup of tea.

21 Afterword

In 1989, a few days after the fall of the Berlin Wall, Marvin Jacks read about her in a syndicated newspaper column. A young reporter in Madison, Wisconsin had learned about her years before that, but the CIA convinced his paper to hold the story, not only for national security reasons but also for her safety. But when the German Democratic Republic ceased to exist for all practical purposes, there was no reason to hold the story any longer. The problem was that so long after the facts it was no longer a hot story. The reporter had moved on and had become nationally syndicated, so he ran it as human interest directly connected with the fall of the Wall and later, of the German democratic Republic – which had never been either democratic or a republic – which was covering the front pages of the world.

Judith Baumgartner had been living in Madison with her daughter in a defector protection program, working as a German teacher in a Rudolf Steiner Waldorf school, where her daughter was a pupil. The Stasi somehow found out who and where she was – something which was never supposed to happen – and sent a hit man to eliminate her. They were pissed off. As an experienced spy, when she defected, she was able to give the CIA information about the Stasi infrastructure, modus operandi, names, etc. The hit man (let's call him Hans as the reporter unimaginatively did), was on his first job and wasn't really a hit man. They'd sent him because their experienced assassins, knowing that the regime was wobbly, were either disappearing into West Germany or were afraid of getting caught trying to enter the United States so late in the game. Hans, however, had entered the U.S. on several previous occasions on minor missions with a genuine Spanish passport. His father was a Spanish communist and his mother a German one. He was born in East Germany, had attended primary school in Spain and his Spanish was fluent, so he easily passed for the real thing.

Hans wasn't stupid. When he got to Madison, instead of killing Judith he telephoned from a public phone far from his motel and told her who he was and what his mission was and that he had never killed anyone in his life and preferred to join her rather than kill her. She figured that if she refused to help him, he might feel forced to carry out his mission. So, she said *Ja* – and told him to call her the next day. She got in touch with her old buddy Jack Quinn, now a section head (to a large extent thanks to her defection) at Langley. Quinn flew to Madison. So, when Hans rang her doorbell Quinn was sitting there on the couch with a big smile and another agent was behind a curtain with a rifle pointed at the door. A third agent was behind a bush in the garden ready to plug Hans if he were to take out a weapon when she opened the door. It was all unnecessary though. Hans was unarmed and wanted nothing more than to throw himself into the arms of the CIA with defector status.

Until he read the story not even Marvin Jacks knew where she was. At the time of her defection, he had passed up the opportunity to continue as her lover because it could have compromised her and Micaela's safety and, well, maybe this was one too many identities for him to swallow. Life is complicated enough, he told himself. He knew that Quinn had also been hot for her, but that kind of relationship between an agent and a defector is definitely frowned upon by the CIA.

Now, having just separated from another partner who, though beautiful and rich, was boring, Jacks felt that perhaps he had made a mistake. So, he called Jack Quinn and asked him about Judith.

"She left for Germany as soon as the GDR collapsed, Marvin," he said.

"Ah, For good?"

"Looks like it. Seems she's become an anthroposophist, whatever that is. Better than a communist, I guess."

Marvin Jacks had a vague idea of what an anthroposophist is. Herr S-K had bent his ear about it during the time they were waiting for Micaela in the Rudolf Steiner Schule. And later during the long drive from Buenos Aires to Paraguay Anneliese also spoke about it, but in a less fundamentalist way than Herr S-K. It has to do with reincarnation and karma, something he'd been interested in since reading about it, but not the Indian version, according to which you can reincarnate in animals. Since she worked as a teacher in a Steiner school (called "Waldorf" in the U.S.) in Madison, she might well do the same in Germany. But where? Marvin decided that Herr S-K of the Rudolf Steiner Schule in Florida, Province of Buenos Aires, might be able to give him a hint.

On the following morning, a pleasant Spring day, which he took as a good omen, he entered the school's office at one o'clock when classes should be letting out and confronted Frau Fincklefrick. When she said that Herr S-K was busy and asked what he wanted to see him about, he decided that she was the kind of German who only understood orders. *"Sagen Sie Herrn S-K dass ich hier bin und dringend mit ihm sprechen muss — sofort!"* he shouted. She jumped up like a scared rabbit. "Jawohl, mein herr." and rolled out the door. A minute later Herr S-K entered looking worried. I glanced severely at Frau F, who bowed out and closed the door. Naturally Herr S-K wanted to know about Micaela and her mother. I told him that they had returned to Germany now that the GDR no longer existed, and Marie had loved his school so much that she wanted to be a teacher in one. Could he give her advice on how to go about it?

"In Germany?" he exclaimed. "She must go to the Waldorf Teachers Training Seminar in Stuttgart we send our own teachers there." He grasped Marvin's hand, surprising him with his strength. "Das ist wunderbar! Can you tell her? Are you going to Germany too?" Jacks said, truthfully, that he expected to visit Germany soon and would certainly tell her.

By the time he reached his house he had it mostly figured out. He dived into the pool and floated. He would fly to Germany on Friday. A weekend jaunt wouldn't do, though. He'd have to take a few days' vacation time. In Frankfurt he'd rent a car on Sunday. No, he'd go by one of Germany's excellent trains; there must be several a day from Frankfurt to Stuttgart. On Monday morning he'd be in the Waldorf Teachers Training Seminar, where he'd ask for ... who? Her real name of course. He was confident she'd be there. After all, how could two people be thrown together repeatedly in such unusual circumstances without it being their mutual destiny ... or, rather, karma, as Judith would say? First in San Francisco as Olga the Russian; then as Anneliese the East German, then in Buenos Aires as Frau Marie, the West German. He had been in love with all those incarnations. Now the time had come to know and love Judith -- ex-spy, communist, anthroposophist: the real thing.

Despite the demise of the Soviet Union, spying has not lost its allure, nor, as far as we know, has love.

About the author

Frank Thomas Smith is an American expatriate who has lived most of his adult life in Europe (Switzerland, Germany) and South America (Argentina) During his career in the Airline industry he moonlighted in education (Waldorf), translating and writing. What was once moonlighting is now full-time. He lives in the mountains in Argentina.

ANTHROPOSOPHICAL FANTASIES (by Roberto Fox, as told to Frank Thomas Smith): Anthroposophy, also known as Spiritual Science, is not known for fantastic literature, or fiction at all. So how can stories with titles like "Life on Mars," or "The Girl in the Floppy Hat," or "To Hunt a Nazi" qualify as anthroposophical. They do not — until now. Therefore, this book is groundbreaking. You may smile at times, even laugh; other stories may cause a lump in your throat ...
ISBN: 978-1948302104

ANTHROPOSOPHICAL GUIDELINES (Rudolf Steiner, translated by Frank Thomas Smith): this volume contains a collection of short essays by Steiner for the members of the Anthroposophical Society. They were written near the end of Steiner's life and in a way summarize, in highly concentrated form, the whole of anthroposophy. Each essay ends with a short summary of its contents and these are known, in this translation, as the "guidelines." The guidelines are mantras and can be used quite fruitfully for meditation. Frank Thomas Smith provides a new, reinvigorated translation of Rudolf Steiner's classic, "Anthroposophical Leading Thoughts."
ISBN: 978-1948302418

CORONAVIRUS PANDEMIC II (by Judith von Halle, translated by Frank Thomas Smith): In this book, the main focus is not on the distressing social developments that have arisen as consequence of the coronavirus pandemic – and for good reason: Although there are already (thankfully) many quality descriptions and articles about this complex of problems and questions, at the same time on the other hand a dangerous knowledge-vacuum has arisen. Therefore, in this book I will refrain from elaborating on the problems already made widely visible in favor of this knowledge-vacuum, which will be outlined as an addition to what has already been described in Vol. I.
ISBN: 978-1948302357

ESOTERIC LESSONS FOR THE FIRST CLASS Volumes I, II, and III (Rudolf Steiner, translated by Frank Thomas Smith): During the re-founding of the Anthroposophical Society at Christmas 1923, Rudolf Steiner also reconstituted the 'Esoteric School' which had originally functioned in Germany from 1904 until 1914, when the outset of the First World War made it's continuance impossible. Twenty-eight lectures in three Volumes with in-line illustrations and blackboard drawings.
ISBN: 978-1948302289 (vol. 1), 978-1948302302 (vol. 2), 978-1948302333 (vol. 3)

FAVELA CHILDREN (by Ute Craemer, translated by Frank Thomas Smith): Ute Craemer is an educator and social worker who has dedicated over fifty years of her life to teaching and nurturing the poor children of the favelas (slums) in Brazil. As an experienced Waldorf teacher, she has been able to understand the needs of the children and their families and provide them with the spiritual nourishment they cry out

for. Favela Children is a moving and informative account of Ute's Craemer's social work in the favelas and of her personal development ...
ISBN: 978-1948302425

THE HISTORY AND ACTUALITY OF IMPERIALISM (Rudolf Steiner, translated by Frank Thomas Smith): In 1920 Rudolf Steiner had already foreseen that the future imperialism would be economic rather than military or nationalistic. In these three lectures he describes the history of imperialism from ancient times to the present and into the future. The Anglo-American would play an increasingly important role in future developments, so the English visitors who attended must have been especially attentive.
ISBN: 978-1948302203

JOURNEY TO THE STARS (by Frank Thomas Smith): The protagonists of these 12 stories are involved in fascinating adventures, which will delight young readers and leave an indelible impression on their minds and hearts. For children from 9 years old on up.
ISBN: 978-1948302395

THE MAGIC MOUND (by Frank Thomas Smith): Sergio and his younger brother, Divino are poor children who live in a favela (slum) in Sao Paulo, Brazil. They go on vacation with their revered teacher, dona Ute (pronounced oo-teh), to the country house of one of Ute's friends. Once there, they leave the house together to fetch kindling wood. They cross a stream and discover a strange round mound surrounded by white stones ... for children from 9 years old on up.
ISBN: 978-1948302258

THE TALKING TREES / LOS ÁRBOLES PARLANTES (by Frank Thomas Smith): Alma and Nico live on opposite ends of a forest near their homes. One day when they are both reading the same book (The Magic Mound) within the forest, but far from each other, the trees suddenly talk to them. A bilingual edition for children from 9 years old on up.
ISBN: 978-1948302715

TOWARD A THREEFOLD SOCIETY (Rudolf Steiner, translated by Frank Thomas Smith): This work, written late in the life of Rudolf Steiner, makes use of a threefold analysis of the human individual and of human society. Man as an individual, or in a group, functions basically in three modes: thinking/perceiving, feeling/valuing, and willing/planning/acting. A unit of functioning, whether a part of an individual or part of a society has its proper role. Each role needs a certain respect from other areas if it is to function properly ...
ISBN: 978-1-948302-16-6